MIMIKA AVENUE

A Novel By

Allysha Hamber

MIMIKA AVENUE®

MIMIKA AVENUE

Is a work of fiction. Any resemblances to real people, living or dead, actual events, establishments, organizations, or locales are intended to give the fiction a sense of reality and authenticity. Other names, characters, places and incidents are either products of the author's imagination or are used fictitiously. Those fictionalized events & incidents that involve real persons did not occur and/or may be set in the future.

Written by: Allysha Hamber
Edited by: Wendy Robinson
Cover design by: Tony Lockett
Email: crocodilelounge@aol.com

For information contact:
Allysha Hamber
Email: Lele4you@hotmail.com
Allysha4you@hotmail.com
Website: www.myspace.com/allyshahamber
Facebook.com/allyshahamber

ISBN: 1448666953

Dedication

This book, as with every positive thing I do in life, is for my babies... my children, Dorian Jones (You are so much like me that it both scares me and soothes me. I know you are a survivor but you'll always be my baby. Never give up and never stop dreaming. I have so much faith in you even when you don't have it in yourself!), Davion and Tamara Hamber. My heart will always, always belong to you! Momma loves you very, very much! Nothing or no one has the power to ever change that!

To those who are so special to me. Never changing, never judgmental but always full of genuine love and encouragement.

Shouts Out...

First and foremost, to my Heavenly Father for allowing me a chance to do it again... I Thank You with all my heart! My nieces ... Quionna, Miracle, Taderra & Meka. My nephews'... CJ, Chris & Cory and Lil' Ty. My first Great nephew... Semaj. My God-nieces... Wendy Robinson, Rosetta Bonner and Shavonna Bonner (I know I got a lot more but it's too many of ya'll. Know that I love you all though!) My babies from another mother... Jazmine Bonner, Jordan Bonner, Justice Arties and Jada Bonner. My sisters... Sherri Jones, Maria Jones, LaNelle Jackson-Jones, Rhonda Jones, Vincell Jones. My Brothers... Christopher Jones, Wayne Jackson, Salt, Uncle Mont, Uncle Fred and Uncle Quinton. I love you all!

To my Peoples: Issac Bonner (My Nigga... you always been real.. Love Ya!), Lorraine Bonner (Thanks for always telling me the things I never want to hear! Love Ya!), Sylvester & Venita Dixon, Da Mo2vata (Bluer then blue), Jayson Lambert, Shannon Rucker (Miss you!), Jean Whitby (Hey Sissy... Thanks for all your love and support.) Momma Whitby (Love ya!), Antoine Anderson, (Thank you for all your love and support.) Beverly Shelton, George Spates (Hold Me Down!) TB & the fellas at TB'S Barber Shop...Chuck Deizel and Yaya (Always glad you guys are apart of my life!)

To Guy Bonner: You have certain qualities that God have blessed you with, that in turn, blesses' me and others. Thank you for allowing me to share in your life, your children's life and your family's life. May God continue to shine down upon you and all you do! I Love You!

Last but certainly not least... to those who have made living on "Mimika" one of the best experiences of my life... I thank you! Without ya'll, this book wouldn't be possible... Get Down, Harvey, Darnell, DC, Lil' Curtis, Tee-Tee, Bruce, RJ, Unc (love you!), Cocamo (You know that as long as I have breath in my body... I will always love you! You will always be one-of-a-kind in my eyes! Thanks for letting me write my feeling for you!) Toi, Hank, Man and everybody else that gave me something to write about...Much Love!

4

FOREWORD
By
Antoine Anderson, STL's HumbleWriter's

Welcome, as I take your mind and spirits on a journey...
To the best story ever told, listen up and you'll learn the hood.
All the way from Gators and Now & Laters; to thunder cats
and now-haters. Welcome, this is Mimika !!!

See it sits in da Lou, home of da Apple Bottom's and what-nots,
I swear this block holds all the nigga's, that care not!!! See each
one has a struggle within their own, for age holds no gravity here.
They shakin' and serving from da payphones, fuck fear!!!!!!

Welcome, this is Mimika, where a slew of nigga's share the
corners, that's real. Where Nine Millimeter slugs chase mahogany
skin, cuz that skin, is chasin' pills. A street full of meds like the
doctor's home, where even grandma claps back, if u don't leave
her alone!!!

See the coldest winter here, is a hustle with no direction and a
wanksta is one, who has to hustle his or her own reflection.
Did I mention? This is Mimika... the heart of the hood, where
everybody's up to no good, or so it would seem to an outsida.

Step on this block, only if you can bare the heat, in the belly of the
beast and bring the noise, only if you can withstand the loudness
retuned to your ear drums, like mesmerizing bass to a song.

On this block, they go hard in da paint and the blood drips
continuously into the sewer; where it travels to the river and on to
other parts of the world and so fallen soldiers, live on and on and
on...

Stroke my ego, ya know, I'ma take a break to ya'll catch up
and re-up, TURN THE PAGE for passion and pain!!!!!!!!!!!!!!
Welcome to Mimika ....

Hood Love
By
Krazy Rythmn, the Poet

What does this title mean to you?
Is it the power that you bring to your crew?

-OR-

Does highlights, run through your mind, of the way you shine,
Proud of the depths, in which you grind?

Could it be the respect that you get, from the guidelines that you set?

-OR-

Is it the set you claim?

The crime that everyone knows you committed
Yet, honoring the street code, it went un-blamed.

-OR-

The fact you have the knack, to give back
Due to the finances you got, that most lack

-OR-

How about this?
Is it... **NONE OF THE ABOVE!**

The unknown, the unexpected
What no hood figure is thinking of?

The one to never beg, they keep a lil' change
They stay out yo' business but stimulate yo' business brain

The one who holds it down, while you running all around town
To return home, not to a sound nor a frown

-NOW-

I MUST ASK YOU THIS, ONCE AGAIN....
WHAT DO YOU THINK OF WHEN YOU HEAR THE TITLE OF THIS
POEM.... **HOOD LOVE?**

Prelude

Seven am on one of the Walnut Park neighborhood's hottest mornings, Cocamo stepped onto his discolored brick porch with his arms stretched wide, inhaling the smoggy air of Mimika Avenue. He pulled up one of the off white, plastic chairs, reached in his pocket, pulled out his cigarettes and lit up a Newport.

Cocamo was Walnut Parks' neighborhood version of Martin's *hustle man*. Any and everything you could want or need, he could get it for you. Need a TV, call Cocamo. Need a transmission for your car or an air conditioner for your crib, call Cocamo. Need gun play; you could call him for that too.

Standing all of Six-foot-two inches tall, two hundred and one pounds, caramel-skinned, with a Spider cut fade and his face neatly trimmed, Cocamo was a handful with the ladies.

The neighborhood *chicken-heads* flocked to him like flies to shit, but Cocamo was a business man and he heavily believed in MOB (Money-over-bitches). He never put anyone before his money, especially a piece of pussy.

Cocamo was an all around good guy from the hood. He'd help you out if he could but if you should so happen to get on his bad side, look out. He had mad artillery and he was down for poppin' his nine when necessary.

As he puffed his nerve calmer, Cocamo called out to the local neighborhood dope man as he exited his '01 tan and chrome Suburban truck across the street.

"Aey nigga! It's time fo' that medication."

"It's good my cat, just gimme one sec, I got you," the man answered, turning up his favorite liquid beverage, an ice cold tall can of Bud Light.

Spider was everybody's favorite herb specialist. He had the fattest bags around and he always believed in sharing his wealth with those closest to him.

Standing five-eleven, two hundred and twenty five pounds, mocha complexion, with broad shoulders, Spider was hood to the bone. His braids, long in length and stayed designed in the latest styles. His calf-length Phem shorts, starched fresh from the cleaners and his thigh length white tee, creased sharply down the center. His legs were slightly bowed and sported his war wounds of the past. His arms, flossing the tattoo's of the Jeff Vanderlou (JVL) set he claimed as a youth.

Spider walked onto the porch of the run down, one family unit located at the corner of Mimika and Harney Avenue. He sat down his Bud Light and gave hood love to his home boys, Tank, Get Down and DC, sitting on the porch. It was their every morning routine, meeting on the front porch with the rise of the sun, to have a drink amongst the crew.

"Aey, Spider, man you hear about that cat that got popped last night over on Lucille," DC asked him.

"Who?"

"Shit, Hawk 'nem laid that nigga Slick down sideways, you heard me," DC said, hitting the half pint of grape MD 20/20 on the bottom with his palm before popping the top.

He passed the bottle around so that all the crew, could do the same.

"These nigga's gon' learn to quit fuckin' with muthafucka's shit. Slick broke into Hawk's 'nem house the night before last and stole all kinds of shit. Even the muthafuckin' copper out the basement. Hawk 'nem followed his ass from F&G's last night and stretched his ass out. Heard they shot all the nigga's fingers off before they shot him in the head," Get Down said, taking a swallow of the purple wine.

"Damn, these nigga's ain't playin'. They lettin' them bells ring around this bitch like it ain't shit," Spider said, reaching down the front of his shorts to retrieve his weed from underneath his balls.

"Hol' on, I gotta go handle somethin'."

Spider walked across Mimika Avenue to the brown and white brick home where Cocamo was sitting on the porch with his uncle.

"What's good, Cocamo? What's good, Unc?" Spider said, as he climbed the steps and gave them love.

"My nigga," Cocamo said, as he reached in his pocket for a twenty dollar bill. Spider watched as Cocamo peeled the twenty dollar bill from a thick wad of cash.

"Damn nigga, the boy business keepin' you fat ain't it?"

"Uhh, basically," Cocamo said, smiling.

They exchanged goods and Spider took a seat on the edge of the porch rail. As Spider sat chit-chatting with his neighbors and customers, gun shots rang out.

Pop, pop, pop, pop.

They all hit the porch ground. Bullets in the hood know no faces and they definitely have no names written on them. The sounds of the screeching tires and the silence of the firecracker sounds in the air, let them know the drama was over...or so they thought.

"Damn, did ya'll hear them shots," the voice asked as they all stood to their feet, dusting off their clothes. They turned to greet their neighbor, Punkin, as she stood in the doorway of her grey and black home.

Punkin was the perfect neighbor, if you lived in the hood because she was simply just "*ghetto by nature.*" She was the kind of neighbor that you could sit around and chill with, smoke a couple of blunts, get your drink on and get all the latest gossip, all

9

at the same time.

She was always in the mist of things. Punkin was so nosey, you didn't need to watch the news or pick up the Evening Whirl to find out information on what went down in the hood. All you had to do was show up, ready to smoke and get an entire ear full.

"DAMN," Spider said as he brushed the porch dirt off his white-tee.

"Who the fuck poppin' that thang this damn early in the mornin'?"

"Aey ya'll, it's a nigga lyin' on the lot over there next to Lil' Curtis 'nem house," Punkin said, pointing to the corner of Mimika and Shulte.

You could see the man's legs stretched out sideways in the patchy grass field. Everyone started walking down to the sidewalk as a crowd began to gather at the corner. Get Down, Tank and DC came running across the block to make sure their home boy was alright.

"Shit nigga, we thought you was toast!" DC said, hitting Spider on the back.

"Fuck that! The only thing toast round this muthafucka, is my drank! A nigga dropped it when them rounds went off."

Spider reached for the MD in DC's hand, turned it up and took it straight to the head. As he turned back towards the porch, out the corner of his eye, he saw her.

Standing on Punkin's steps with her hair pulled up in a ponytail, dressed in soft pink Capri's and a pink floral camisole, was Punkin's youngest sister, Mystic.

Spider had seen her before when he'd brought medicine over to Punkin and her crew but for the most part, they had never said much to each other past "hi and bye."

Mystic was gorgeous to him. Five-five, 160 pounds of thickness, beautiful skin, pretty hands and gorgeous feet. Spider loved a woman with pretty feet. He couldn't stand a woman to wear sandals in the summer time with jacked up feet, lookin' like she'd been busting concrete with her heels.

Mystic waved to him as she came down the steps.

"Hey mommy," Spider said.

"Hey, Spider, what happened?" she asked, approaching him.

"Some nigga got popped."

"In broad daylight?" she asked, folding her arms.

Mystic found the hood life so exciting. She was used to the living the life of a sheltered military wife and mother. Used to the type of neighborhoods where people left their front doors wide open all night and no one would step foot inside their homes. Although the best environment for raising a family, she hated the staleness of the military life and Mystic longed for a life filled with excitement and adventure.

She wanted a "soldier..," not Uncle Sam's illegitimate sons but a real soldier... a hood nigga, a thug-a-boo (a thug-a-boo is a nigga whose gutta on the outside but soft on the inside when it come to his woman). Mystic wanted someone to protect her and make her feel safe. Someone she could share her deepest secrets with and know that he'd make it his business to make it better. Someone who bore the word "Strength" across their chest like a finely pinned tattoo.

Mystic had been peeping Spider since she'd been home and she felt that she saw all the things she wanted in Spider, yet she was also afraid of him. Afraid of some of the bullshit she had heard about him, afraid of the life style everyone said he led. She was afraid mostly because she was already on federal probation and couldn't risk going back to prison for anyone or any reason, no matter how fine he was.

Mystic longed to get her daughter back, the one taken from her when she was arrested eight years ago. Her daughter was only two years old when Mystic last laid eyes on her and she missed her terribly. Mystic had allowed her ex-husband to talk her into going a check cashing scam that went bogus and ended up yielding her six and a half years away from those she loved the most. Getting her daughter back would take Mystic, jumping through many hoops and walking a line so straight, stumbling to the left or the right even slightly, could cost her, her daughter forever.

She couldn't risk getting into trouble again for anyone. She had to stay clean, even if that meant fighting the desire for the streets and her dream of both loving and being loved by a bad boy.

"Well mommy, that's how it goes down in the hood. Gangsta shit don't respect no time of day," Spider said, touching her arm.

Mystic felt a tingle go down her spine. She sank down into his touch.

"Umm, should I go call for help?"

"Naw, I'm sure somebody already did. I'll tell you what you should do, you should let me take you to dinner cause, I think I like you."

Mystic smiled.

She looked Spider in his eyes and wondered if he could see her body crying out to him.

"Really? Yeah, well, I think I like you too but I can't let you take me to dinner," Mystic said, thinking to herself, *damn this nigga is so fucking fine.*

"Why not?"

"Cause," she paused. "You're a bad boy Spider, I can't mess with you. I say probation and your lifestyle is like playin' Russian roulette with my freedom and I ain't tryin' to see them Feds again," she said, walking away.

Spider grabbed her by the arm.

"Mommy. I would never have you around anything that I do. I would never jeopardize you in any way, trust that. You think I wanna see you caged in again? Now, take my number and call me."

Mystic mind told her to walk away again but her body and the overwhelming thirst to know what it felt like to be loved by a thug, controlled her. She took out her cell phone and recorded his number inside.

"Gon' inside, you don't need to be around this shit and nigga's round here believe in round trip tickets," he told her.

"Round trip?" Mystic looked at him confused.

"Meanin', they might round that muthafuckin' corner and slide through again. Especially if they wanna make sure that nigga dead."

She turned to walk away and smiled to herself. Mystic liked the way he had just commanded her to go indoors; she liked the forcefulness in his voice. She turned back to him and waved as she went inside.

"Aey Spider, nigga that's Kay Kay stretched out on that lot," Get Down said, out of breath from running across the street.

"What? My nigga, Kay Kay?"

"Yep. Looks bad too man," he told Spider.

Spider sprinted across the street as Mystic watched him through the window. When he reached his friend, Spider kneeled down and lifted his upper body upon his lap.

13

"My cat, what's good?"

Kay Kay gave no response. He gripped Spider's left arm and opened his mouth to speak but the only thing escaping from his lips was a gush of blood. Kay Kay squeezed Spider's arm tighter and tighter. He was gasping for air as the blood flowed from his body. He had been shot in the stomach, the left leg and his right shoulder.

He was dying right there in Spider's arms.

"Who did this man? Who did this shit to you? Answer me... Kay, answer me."

Kay Kay's signs of life were slipping, fast. Spider felt a tear fall from his eyes as he watched his childhood friend's life slip away. Kay Kay was dead and Spider was in rage. He wiped the blood from his hand onto his shirt and closed his friend's eyes.

He vowed to his friend that he would find out who was responsible and make them pay. No matter when, no matter where he found them, he would make them pay...on that you could bet.

Chapter One

Tee-Tee placed the freshly crisp twenty dollar bill she'd just made into her back Apple Bottom jean's pocket. It had been a good night for her. The block had brought her close to four hundred dollars and now, she was tired. She wanted to simply go home and crash for a couple hours but as her hip began to vibrate and the familiar number flashed across the Nextel screen, she knew that wouldn't be possible, not anytime soon.

"I need you to take a ride with me," the raspy voice came over her earpiece.

"Nigga, I'm tired. I been out here all night grindin'. Call somebody else or see if Lil' Curtis will ride with you."

Tee-Tee stepped out onto the curb and saw the burgundy and gold chromed Escalade pull up to the corner. The driver, a rough looking, pudgy nigga named Big Slug.

Big Slug was a grimy, low down nigga who made his money on the street by any means necessary. He didn't care how he got it or who he had to hurt to get it. His blood bled green and his heart pumped greed.

Tee-Tee, like most of the young gunners in the hood worked for Big Slug. And although she wanted a different life for herself, she knew that it would only be death that could break the hood bond between her and Big Slug. Death... hers or his.

"Nigga, why you do that dumb ass shit? If you knew you was gon' roll up on a bitch, why the fuck did you call?" she asked, lifting her five foot-two inch, 120 pound frame, up into the passenger side of the truck. The tan leather seat felt so soft against her skin. The a/c blowing a cool, refreshing breeze across her sweaty face and chest could have easily put her sleep right then and there.

It was the longing for the plush material things like Big Slug's Escalade that kept Tee-Tee out on the grind all night. She was the only female in the crew of hustler's on the block. And the nigga's gave her the same respect as the other nigga's doing their thing in the hood. She had the same ambitions as them, the same heart as them and the same needs as them. The need to belong to the hood's most elite, the need to both come up and stay up.

"Loyalty T-baby, that's what it's all about. I wanted to see if you was gon' lie to me and tell me you was into somethin' else. Cause if I can't trust you, you dead weight to me and you know how a nigga likes to get rid of dead weight."

Tee-Tee crossed her legs and rolled her eyes out the window as she listened to Big Slug with disgust. *Fake ass Suge Knight,* she thought to herself.

"So, this is what I need. This nigga named Cocamo been hornin' in on my neighborhood action. He been runnin' his mouth, braggin' and shit about he about to take over mines. I want you to get close to him, get up under him, no matter what it takes and take him out. You feel me?"

"And how the fuck am I suppose to do that," she asked. "You know damn well that nigga stay on top of his game."

Big Slug grabbed Tee-Tee's left thigh and pulled it towards him.

"Use what you bitches know best," he said, nodding between her legs.

Tee-Tee pushed away his hand and frowned. Big Slug just snickered at her, knowing Tee-Tee's greed would talk her into going through with it.

"He'll be over on Thekla later on this evening, at that nigga Bo's crib," he said pulling over to the curb in front of her house.

"Now, get the fuck out my truck and get some sleep. I expect results no later than the end of the week."

16

Tee-Tee climbed out of the truck and slammed the door. She hated working for Big Slug but he was one of the biggest player's on the north side. When the streets were running dry, Big Slug somehow always kept them supplied. To Tee-Tee, that meant she could always get money.

So what if she had to put up with a nigga she secretly hated, money ruled the world and she made a promise to get it any way she could.

She turned the key to the front small framed wooden door and entered the house to the sounds of her mother, Yvette asking her once again, where the hell she'd been all night.

"It ain't my job to take care of yo' daughter. Yeah, she's my gran'daughter but I'm not her momma, you are and you need to start actin' like it," Yvette said, as she placed a bowl of dry cereal in front of the one-year-old baby girl.

"Momma, I be out all night, tryin' to make money to take care of Tasha and you. You can't work with a bad back and you know yo' disability check ain't enough to pay nothin' around here. So I gotta do what I gotta do. I don't know 'bout you but I'm tired of not havin' nothin'. My daughter ain't gon' grow up like I did, in all them hand-me-downs and shit."

"You watch yo' damn mouth! You may think you grown but you ain't grown enough to disrespect me, I don't give a damn what you pay."

Yvette walked over to her daughter and placed her hand around Tee-Tee's face. She saw so much of herself as a youth, in her daughter.

"All I'm askin' is for you to try and get a real job and get outta these streets. Get more than a job, get a career, go back to school and do this the right way. These streets are gon' eat yo' ass alive, believe me when I tell you that. If you can't do it for yourself, then do it for Tasha. She deserves to have her momma in her life full-time, not part-time."

Tee-Tee pushed away from her mother's touch and looked off to the wall.

"A regular job ain't gon' get me what me or Tasha need and it shol' ain't gon' get me what I want."

Tee-Tee walked away and headed down the multi-colored hallway to her room. Yvette shook her head and yelled after her, "Yeah well, I know what them streets gon' get you, two things, dead or in jail. And don't call me for no bail money cause I see you gotta learn things the hard way. Well, be my guest but you won't drag my grand-baby down that road with you."

Tee-Tee slammed the bedroom door and plopped down on her squeaky full sized bed. She scanned the walls and frowned at the peeling paint, the water stained ceiling and her ten year old scratched up bedroom furniture. Being inside that room burned her on the inside and it fed her hunger for better things.

Ain't that a bitch, now she wanna be a mother. Fuck that, I'm gon' grind 'til I come up and keep grindin to stay up, no matter what it takes.

With that, she turned on the small white desk fan on the night stand, leaned back on the pillow and went to sleep. She had work to do later that night and nothing or no one would stand in her way of getting what she wanted...hood status.

Chapter Two

Through the window, Mystic watched as Spider emerged from the crowd of on-lookers. The police had taped off the lot and the Coroner had just taken away Kay Kay's body. His crisp white-tee was now soaked with his home boy's blood. Tank, DC and Get Down were close on his tracks, patting him on his shoulder.

Spider reached back, grabbed the MD and finished it off. He threw the bottle across the street in the alley and watched as it shattered on the concrete.

Mystic could feel his pain. From what she had overheard, they were good friends. She opened the door and stared as Spider and his crew passed by her. For a brief moment, their eyes locked and Mystic wanted to run to him and throw her arms around him. She knew the pain of losing someone close to you, all to well.

Instead, she stood idle as he disappeared onto the porch across the way.

"Why you all up in the door like you scared to come outside or something," Punkin asked as she walked into the house to get her cell phone and call someone, anyone to tell her latest gossip too.

"I just wanted to come inside, it seems pretty hectic out there."

"Girl, this is everyday, all day over here. You betta get use to it and if you ain't strong enough to deal with it, you betta fake it. Cause these bitches and nigga's can smell fear and weakness a mile away and trust, they will try you. Unless...unless you down with the set or you got a nigga they fear, to protect you. A real nigga... like, like that," she said, pointing one of the neighborhood hotties, Cocamo, who was walking back onto his porch.

Mystic glanced over as Spider pulled off the blood soaked t-shirt, exposing a strong and powerful chest. She had to admit to herself that living on Mimika would be a challenge for her after coming from such a confined and controlled environment. The hood was buck wild and had a no-holds-barred atmosphere. Yet, Mystic was intrigued by the hood and its people, especially Spider.

She pulled out her cell phone and strolled down the contacts until she reached his number. As she heard the phone ring in her ear, her stomach swirled in butterflies.

"What's good," his voice came blaring over the receiver.

"I just called to see if you were alright."

"Who dis," Spider questioned.

"Look across the street."

Mystic waved to him.

"Yeah, I'm cool. But them nigga's is gon' pay fo' what just went down. You can't touch one of mine and think you gon' get a pass. Fuck an eye fo' an eye. You touch just one of mines, on err thing I love, I'm comin' back fo' all yours."

Mystic smiled to herself, loving the way he talked. He seemed so rough and ghetto. It touched her deep in places she thought was dead. Made her mommy tingle and her heart throb.

Every time she saw him walking towards the house to serve Punkin, her clit would begin to throb just at the very sight of him. His swagger did something erotic and hypnotizing to her body. Now, the sound of his voice was doing the same.

What is it about this nigga? I don't even like sex and I never experienced an orgasm in my life. Now here this nigga come along and got my body trippin' and shit.

"Anyway," Spider continued.

"Shouldn't you be gettin' ready for work?"

"How do you know..."

"This my hood, I know everything," he stated.

"Besides, I been peepin' you."

Mystic smiled again.

"Get dressed, I'll take you."

Before she could answer, he hung up the phone in Mystic's ear.

Damn he bold, I like that shit.

As Mystic dressed for work, she thought back over her life. The ups and the downs, the highs and the Spiders. She couldn't understand how she had ended up here at this point in her life.

Her life, while rough in the beginning, had promise in the later years. Mystic believed that when she had gotten married and moved away from Saint Louis and all the pain that it had brought her, that she would be okay. Maybe pursue her dream of being a writer or a poet.

She was wrong. Things had gotten worse, much worse. The mind games, the cheating and the beatings she had suffered at the hands of her ex-husband had caused her to lose the one person she loved most in life, her daughter, Tia.

Mystic was prosecuted by the Feds for writing bad checks out of bogus checking accounts on a federal installation. Her ex-husband had put her onto the game but was always smart enough not put his hands on any documents. So when the game got twisted and Mystic was arrested, it all fell on her shoulders and like so many before, he hung her out to dry, alone.

It didn't matter that he would smack her around if she didn't do what he wanted, all that mattered to them was that he was one of their own, a soldier. His only concern, was protecting his career in the Marines. At first, she thought of prison confinement as a death sentence but with time, Mystic began to use the time to learn about herself and her relationships with men.

Mystic realized that what she wanted from men was to feel that same love and protection she had felt as a small child before her father left and went to prison on a life sentence. She also came to realize that her search to fill that need in her life, had often led her into the arms of men who used that weakness to control her, violate her and misuse her.

Mystic both wanted and needed to fill that void in her life and felt that on her own, it would never come. But as she saw the tan Suburban pull up in front of her house, she trotted down the steps, hoping she had finally found it, in Spider.

As she closed the passenger side door and turned to thank him for the ride, Mystic noticed the black, shiny nine millimeter lying on his lap and it startled her.

Spider noticed her facial expression and opened the middle console between the seats and placed the gun down inside. He looked at her and placed his hand on her thigh.

"You don't never have to be scared when you with me, Boo. I keep that with me cause of what I do. These lil' cats out here ain't playin' and I ain't gon' end up like my boy did this mornin', you hear me? I stay strapped and you bets believe, when I see them muthafucka's, it's like that."

Mystic sat back in her seat and nodded her head. Everything about him spoke to her soul, forced her to take notice and she loved it. It turned her on that he was so *gutta*. She wanted to take off all her clothes right there and fuck him in the front of the Suburban but instead, she reached down in her purse, lit a Black & Mild and tapped her fingers to his booming system.

"*...yippie-ki-yo, yippie-ki-yea, wanna bump yo' body baby. Wanna bump yo body, wanna bump yo' body. Out on the dance I'm holdin' you so tight, gotta make you feel me, gotta press yo' body tight. Rub against my body grind cause I'm in the mood for the same. Dancin' real freaky, this is how we groove...*"

22

As the Suburban swerved through the neighborhood, Mystic felt important riding beside the man everyone seemed to know and love. When the truck came to a stop in front of the Walgreen's Drug Store, Spider turned down the music and looked to Mystic, "Does it bother you what I do?'

"I mean, I guess you gotta do what you gotta do to survive. It ain't like I don't know how hard it is to get a job out here," she answered.

"Well, I don't sell dope to floss or be a big shot. I do what I do to maintain, nothin' more."

"I understand," she said, exiting the Suburban and walking around to the driver side door.

As Mystic leaned in to kissed him on his cheek, Spider grabbed her underneath her chin and pulled her lips to his. Mystic felt a shiver down her spine and thought to herself, *How can such a hard ass nigga have such soft, sexy ass lips?*

Spider leaned back in the seat and stared at her. She felt so self-conscious and intimidated in his presence. She looked away to the ground.

"Aey mommy," he said, raising her face to him once more. "You gon' be mines, I'ma see to that."

Mystic smiled.

"Now go on to work," Spider told her as his hip began to vibrate. He glanced at the number. "I gotta take this, its business. What time you get off?"

"Ten."

"I'll be here," he said, watching her cross in front of the truck.

As Mystic disappeared inside, Spider answered his phone.

"What's good?"

"Where the fuck you at?" the female voice blared through his Bluetooth.

"At the store, why?"

"Cause I asked. What's this I hear about Kay Kay," the loud woman's voice asked.

"Somebody popped him. Why you callin' me, questioning' me about where I'm at? What I tell you about that shit?"

"Cause I'm yo' wife nigga and I can."

"I got another call comin' through," Spider said brushing her off. He hated a nosey, hawking ass woman calling every ten minutes, not wanting a damn thing other than to find out where he was and what he was doing. Calling and listening to his background, trying to hear who's around him. For that reason alone, he kept his calls under a minute long.

"What's good," he answered the other line.

"I know who did it," Get down told him.

"I'm on my way."

Spider swerved out the parking lot and sped down Jennings Station Road back towards the hood. He reached back down inside the console to retrieve his glock.

He thought about the expression on Mystic's face when she saw it lying on his lap. He saw the fear inside her. Truth was, he was feeling her but if he wanted her to be his woman, he was going to have to remove that fear from inside her. His woman had to be strong, had to be able to watch his back at all times.

Spider had never dealt with her kind before. He was used to the hood rats in the neighborhood. Mystic stuck out like a sore thumb to him and that's what made him want her even more.

She was a challenge to him and for a man who was used to getting what he wanted, Spider knew it would only be a matter of time before he'd get her, in every way he wanted her.

But first...he had blood to get and as he puffed on his Newport and cranked up his system, he promised Kay Kay, once again, that he was about to make them nigga's pay with their lives.

Chapter Three

"...Yeah we gon' ride, yeah we bang, yeah we pop thangz... only in St. Louis. Yeah we in da trap, yeah we getting' scratch, yeah we on da map... only in St. Louis. I'm from the hood where da river is pretty and deep behind the scenes where street's is gully and gritty..."

Spider pulled up to the block and hit his partner Perez on the hip. When it was time to do dirt, Perez was the only one Spider could trust to handle business both swift and quickly.

When Young Jeezy's, *"Put On Fo' My City"* call tone ended, Spider began to brief his friend on what was happening.

"Let's get some."

"What's good," Perez answered.

"It's like a dryer with no Bounce sheet, nigga, we got static," Spider told him, as he checked the clip to his glock make sure it was fully loaded.

"I'm on my way, nigga."

Spider placed the gun inside his waist and exited the truck to talk to Get Down and Tank. Tank handed Spider the bottle of Crown Royal and Spider took it to the head as Get Down ran down the names of those responsible for taking the life of his friend.

"Aey nigga, Harvey just told us it was that lil'; dusty ass nigga Curly and his partna' that hit Kay Kay," Get Down said.

"Which one, that nigga Curly with all that muthafuckin' hair on his chest?"

"Yep," Tank chimed in. "You want me to ride down on them nigga's wit' you?"

"Naw man, it's good. Perez is on his way and we at 'em."

"Aey, Spider man, twist them muthafucka's sideways, you hear me? Get down how you live nigga," Get Down told him.

Perez soon pulled on the block and got out his gold-toned Cutlass and showed hood love to his crew. Spider handed him the Crown Royal and began to break down the situation at hand.

"Its simple nigga, follow my lead and when I start shootin', anything that don't run, kill it. Cause if a muthafucka ain't started runnin' when them rounds go off, they ain't got nothin' to lose or somethin' to prove."

"Uhh, basically," Perez told him, as he slapped him some dap.

"Well shit, nigga, I'm drivin' or somethin'," Tank said.

"Aight then, take the plates off the truck and let's mount up," Spider told him.

They stood and finished off the bottle of Crown Royal as Spider's rage grew more and more from the effects of the alcohol. When the bottle was empty, Spider patted the gun on his waist and turned to Perez, "You ready to get some?"

They got into the Suburban and combed the neighborhood streets, searching for their target. The tinted windows on the truck kept them hidden from the snitches on the block. As they turned down Sherry, Spider spotted Curly and his crew, standing on the front porch of a boarded up, vacant house.

Tank parked the truck on the corner as him, Spider and Perez laid out their plan.

"Aight, nigga's," Tank began. "I'ma let ya'll nigga's out on this corner and after ya'll lay these bitch ass nigga's down, cut through the gang way and I'll meet ya'll in the back alley."

Spider handed Perez one of his black braid caps from inside the console. They pulled the stocking's down over their faces and checked their guns one last time before exiting the Suburban.

They ducked down around the back of the truck so they could use the parked cars on the block as cover.

Spider set his feet at the front of the second car, closest to their target. Perez nodded his head to Spider, letting him know that he was ready to handle business.

It was as if *Menace II Society* was filming that day, as Spider stood to his feet and began to let off rounds, simultaneously with Perez's.

Boom, Boom, Boom....

Tat,tat,tat,tat,tat.....

Bodies began to fall as their guts splattered from the hot lead. Perez did exactly as Spider had asked. Everything that didn't move when the first round popped off, he bucked and laid 'em down.

They continued to fire as they moved in closer and closer. When they reach the crew, those that were still alive were squirming all about. Begging and pleading for their lives, including Curly.

Spider stood directly over him and ordered him to turn over and face him. When the blood soaked body didn't respond, Spider unleashed a series of kicks to his mid-section until he complied.

"I told you nigga's, you touch one of mine, I'm comin' back for all yours."

With that, Spider and Perez popped off rounds into all the remaining bodies. Then Perez joined Spider as they both lit off their remaining rounds into Curly with fury. They made sure to leave him unrecognizable to anyone who would even think of attending his funeral.

They wanted their message sent.....*If you think you man enough to bring it to Mimika, make sure you man enough to take it.*

Perez hit Spider on the arm and as planned, they hit the gangway on the side of the house, ran down a few houses and jumped into the Suburban where Tank was waiting.

"Damn nigga's, it sounded like World War III over there, I know ya'll canceled them nigga's," Tank said.

"Like a muthafuckin' bad check," Spider chuckled.

Chapter Four

Tee-Tee tried to calm the butterflies in her stomach as she wrapped the tan leather straps of her high heels, around her calves. She stared at herself in the mirror and frowned.

"This country ass nigga Big Slug is trippin'. The only reason he got me doin' this shit cause his fat ass is scared of Cocamo."

She looked herself over in the mirror.

"Fuck it, it's all about gettin' that paper. Shit, I need the money and it ain't like I ain't never killed a nigga before," she reassured herself as she zipped up her dark brown mini skirt.

She unwrapped and combed her shoulder length hair down over her tan sleeveless top. Tee-Tee had spent most of her teenage years in the juvenile system for killing her father. He had consistently beaten on her mother with fury, week after week as Tee-Tee and her younger sister Quionna stood by help-less. The faithful night his life ended, he had started in on Tee-Tee and her sister.

Tee-Tee still often saw him inside her dreams. His fists, raising towards them, pounding on top of their flesh. His blood... spurting from his body and staining the bright off white walls. His voice, calling them every dirty and volatile name his mind could muster up.

He had just finished pounding on their mother, when Tee-Tee and her sister had gone into the room to help her. His anger quickly turned towards them and Tee-Tee could take no more.

She scurried her thirteen year old frame into the living room, kneeled down and stuck her hand underneath the red velvet sofa to grab the 38 revolver. The gun was heavy to her but somehow, she found the strength to aim it and use it.

When Tee-Tee re-entered the room, her father Sam had just thrown Quionna across the room with a forceful slap from the back side of his hand. When he noticed Tee-Tee in the door way, he just laughed.

"Now what the hell you gon' do with that besides make me even madder, you lil' bitch?"

With shaky hands, Tee-Tee pointed the gun at Sam's abdomen and shouted, "Leave us alone! Don't touch my momma or my sister, no more."

Again, Sam laughed as he lunged towards her with fury. Tee-Tee closed her eyes and squeezed the trigger, letting off two rounds into his body. The sounds of her mother's screams still played in her head sometimes.

When the police arrived, her mother refused to tell the police that she was being abuse because Sam still showed signs of life when the ambulance had taken him from the house. He was also on parole and having a gun in the house would send him back to prison. Abused or not, Yvette couldn't bring herself to turn her back on him like that. Sometimes it's easier to turn it on the weaker one of the situation and she did. She told them that Tee-Tee and her father were arguing and Tee-Tee pulled out the gun to scare him and it went off.

Tee-Tee went along with the story, figuring that since she was just a child; no judge would put her behind bars. But when Sam died, the scenario changed dramatically and Tee-Tee faced the choice of exposing her family's dirty laundry, against her mother's wishes or bow down and do the juvenile time, until she turned eighteen. For her mother and younger sister's sake, Tee-Tee chose the latter.

Tee-Tee often believed that deep down, she and her mother both resented each other for what happened that night. Her mother resented her for killing the man she somehow managed to still love, despite the numerous trips to the hospital with broken arms and jaw bones. Tee-Tee resented her mother for asking her to choose between her freedom and a family secret that would later come out anyway.

The abuse her mother suffered at the hands of her father eventually led to Yvette's disability and Tee-Tee grind. The need for money fed her need to hustle and also regained her focus on the task at hand.

Tee-Tee gave herself a once over and left the house, walked around the block and slowed down about six houses before she got to Cocamo's house. He was sitting on the front porch, doing his thang, as always. When he saw her approaching, he came down off the porch and called her over to him.

"Where the fuck you goin' lookin' all sexy and shit? Damn, you lookin' quite hittable to a nigga right now, girl!"

Tee-Tee smiled.

"You silly, I'm just going over on Hillard and fuck with my peoples, Peaches fo' a minute."

"Ump! Fuck that, you need to come on in and chill with me fo' a minute. You can get up with that bitch later. We can kick back, watch a movie or somethin'. You know I been tryin' to hit that fo' the longest."

She had accomplished step one, he noticed her. Not only did he notice her but invited her inside. That was better than she could have hoped for.

"Maybe I could chill fo' a minute," she responded, patting the silver twenty-two inside her purse. She wasn't stupid though, there was no way she was gonna try Cocamo on his own turf.

Everyone in the neighborhood knew that Cocamo had more artillery inside his home than the Marine Corp. Tee-Tee knew that once she got inside the house, there would be no coming out, not alive anyway if she went through with her plan. She needed to lure him out of his comfort zone. Maybe get him to a motel or something.

It would take way more time than Big Slug wanted, for her to build that kind of bond with Cocamo. But she was up to the challenge and as she followed him up the porch steps and into the house, she quietly sealed the deal with in herself.

Once inside the house, Cocamo offered her a seat on the black leather sofa as he checked her out from head to toe. She sat down, crossed her legs and reached down inside her purse.

"Is it okay if I smoke in here," she asked, holding up the Philly Blunt in her hand.

"Hell yeah, fire that shit up," Cocamo said, walking through the dining room, to the kitchen at the back of the house.

"You want somethin' to drink? We got Patron, Henny and Seagrams Gin."

Cocamo's plan was to smoke a few blunts with Tee-Tee, get her tipsy and fuck the shit out of her. After that, he'd be good on her, he would have no more use for her, just as he did all his other women.

"I'll take a lil' Patron," Tee-Tee answered back.

When Cocamo returned to the living room, Tee-Tee had fired up a blunt and made herself comfortable on the couch. Her legs were now resting on the sofa cushion beside her. Cocamo handed her the drink and sat down beside her. He rubbed his hand against her thigh.

"Damn girl, I don't know why you been so stingy with all this. Keepin' a nigga on hold and shit."

"Boy please, you ain't really been tryin' to get up on this. You been doin' yo' thang; full-time pimpin' and shit. You ain't been tryin' to holla fo' real."

Cocamo took the blunt from Tee-Tee's hand and held it up to his mouth. He inhaled the smoke slowly and let it out with a series of coughs to follow.

"This that nigga Spider shit, ain't it?"

"You know it," Tee-Tee said, as she gulped down her drink and sat the glass on the table. Cocamo liked the way she handled her drink and he smiled to himself, "*Yeah, I'm finna tear this hoe up!*"

He turned on the stereo and pumped up the sounds of T-Pain's, **I'm In Luv With A Stripper**. "*...she grindin', she vibin', she rollin'. She climbin' that pole'n. I'm in luv with a stripper. She trippin', she swayin', she playin', I'm not goin' no where, girl I'm stayin', I'm in luv with a stripper...*"

Tee-Tee, starting to feel the effects of the Patron and weed together, rose up off the couch and began dancing and gyrating to the beat of the music. Cocamo got behind her and rubbed his jimmy against her body, making sure she felt his hardness.

Tee-Tee pushed against him. She wanted to get him hot and bothered. She wanted to take him off his square. She needed to gain his interest and hold it there, in order for her plan to work. She figured if she could somehow seem unique from the rest of his groupies, she could accomplish her goal and lure him away from his safety zone.

Their stubbornness to be out done, kept them constantly trying to out do one another. They drank, smoked and drank some more, until they fell out on the couch. Tee-Tee lay between his legs, with her head against his chest.

Cocamo awakened a few hours later with her arms wrapped around his waist and her heart beating in rhythm with his. He checked his watch, it was Eleven PM.

He looked down at Tee-Tee, sleeping so peacefully upon his chest and Cocamo began to feel a little uncomfortable. He made it a habit, never to become too cozy with any woman. Now, he couldn't understand it, but, apart of him didn't want to wake her. A part of him felt strangely warm, with her against his chest.

34

Yet, eventually the dog in him took over, as he rubbed her head and told her to get up.

"I want that," he told her, as Tee-Tee wiped her hair from her face.

"Want what?"

"That fire I hear you got."

Cocamo pulled his jimmy from his pants and swung it from side to side. He grabbed the back of Tee-Tee's head and guided her down to his awaiting jimmy.

Tee-Tee really wasn't feeling giving Cocamo oral sex because of the volume of women she knew he slept with but she had to get inside his head. She needed to make a statement. So she grabbed his jimmy and went to work. In her head, she told herself that she had to be the best he ever had. And she focused real hard on achieving this as she deep throated his jimmy at will. She came up with a swirling motion, wet from her saliva and then dropped down on it with a forceful sucking motion, swallowing her slob and the head of his jimmy at the same time.

Cocamo lay back on the couch amazed that she had it going on the way she did. Had he known it was this good, he would have worked harder to get at her sooner. But Cocamo wasn't into chasing women, women were into chasing him. All of them wanted to be the first lady of a hustler. It gave them hood status.

Cocamo was relaxed, enjoying the way Tee-Tee was making him feel. He thought to himself, "*I hope the pussy feel as good as this head she layin' down.*"

Cocamo pulled her head away from his jimmy and instructed her to take off her skirt. As Tee-Tee began to unlatch her mini skirt, Cocamo changed his mind.

"Leave it on."

He stood up, walked to the back of the house to his bedroom and retrieved a Trojan. He came back into the living room, bent Tee-Tee over the arm of the couch, pulled her panties to the side and entered her. She was loose to him but he still liked the way she felt around his jimmy. She got super wet and that was a plus to him. Cocamo hated fucking dry ass pussy.

Tee-Tee gyrated her hips against his body and took in every inch of him. She too, has secretly wanted to know what he felt like for the longest time. She had constantly had heard how good he was and now that she was experiencing it for herself, she made sure she felt every stroke.

"Damn, lil' momma, this pussy good."

"This dick is good, nigga."

Cocamo slapped Tee-Tee on the ass cheek with a forceful thrust as he came close to his climax.

"You gon' swallow this?"

Tee-Tee wasn't into the protein diet but he'd push her away for sure if she resisted. She pulled herself off his jimmy, sat down on the couch, removed his rubber and resumed oral sex.

Cocamo gripped the back of her head and shoved his jimmy to the back of her throat as he released a full load of sperm onto her tonsils. He pumped his body numerous of times, to make sure she had no choice but to swallow every ounce of his juices.

Tee-Tee wanted to gag but instead, she played the role as if she loved it in order to score major points with him. You know nigga's love them women that swallow...

"Damn girl, I'ma need to hit that pussy again someday, real soon."

"Good, cause I'ma need to give it to you again, real soon." Tee-Tee told him, trying her best to talk without swallowing his kids. She was not about to digest all them other bitches' juices.

When Cocamo walked back to the bathroom to clean himself off, Tee-Tee took the opportunity to spit out the milky white substance down between the couch seats. Cocamo returned to the living room with a towel for Tee-Tee. He was outdone at himself for even thinking to bring her one in the first place. He usually didn't care if a hoe went home with sex juices running all down their thighs. But for some reason, he thought of her and he didn't like that, so he quickly re-gained his composure.

"Aight, well, I'm about to go back here and crash. You can clean yo'self off and head on out. I'm sure the block is callin' you."

Tee-Tee, for some reason took offense to his comments, even though she was expecting something foul to come out of his mouth sooner or later. Cocamo was known to be cruel to women after he slept with them. Walk by them on the street and act like he doesn't even know them. Still, her feelings were a little hurt by what he said but she refused to show it. It actually pissed her off, that he felt he could use her like that.

But she kept her cool. She cleaned herself up, gathered her things with finesse, reached down in her purse for a pen and paper to leave him her number and told him whenever he wanted her to break him off again, just holla.

Cocamo came back into the living room once he heard the door close. He picked up the paper off the table and read her note. He looked out the window and watched Tee-Tee walk down the steps. He found himself making sure that she got across the street and onto the block safely.

He picked up the paper again from the brown oak coffee table and chuckled, "What the fuck is wrong me?"

Tee-Tee crossed the street and followed her instincts to look back towards the house. She felt him staring at her and when her suspicions were confirmed, she smiled.

"It's just a matter of time nigga, Queen takes your Rook."

Tee-Tee made it to the block and began her paper chase. Her mind constantly swayed between Cocamo and the grind at hand.

She thought about how good he felt inside of her but she also thought about how taking him out would bring her the hood status she desired for so long.

She was deep in thought, mentally marking her progress, when her hip began to vibrate. It was Big Slug. Tee-Tee sighed and flipped open the cell phone.

"You takin' care of that?" Big Slug asked her.

Tee-Tee frowned and answered, "The game has begun."

Chapter Five

Mystic stood outside the Walgreens store, waiting for the 41 Lee bus to take her home. She was disappointed that Spider hadn't arrived to pick her up but she was use to catching the bus home. She really wanted to see him though. She had waited almost an hour and that was long enough for her.

As she sat on the bus, riding down Riverview Blvd, her cell phone rang. She didn't know which emotion to feel as she saw his number flash across the screen. Her feelings were a little hurt he'd left her stranded but a part of her was also excited.

"Hello?"

"What's good Boo, where you at?"

"On the bus, about to cross McLaran."

"Get off," Spider demanded.

Mystic, without hesitation, pulled the cord to request the next stop and stood at the back door to exit the bus. The tan Suburban swerved directly in front of the bus and Mystic smiled to herself.

She had been waiting to see him all day and even though she was a little upset that he had her waiting for almost an hour, as soon as she laid eyes on him, all that went away. All she could see was him, sitting there, looking so fine to her.

"I got a lil' caught up, that's why I'm so late gettin' to you."

"That's cool, I understand but a phone call would've been nice."

"Aey, sometimes you into shit that won't allow you to make a phone call. Anyway, I'm here now, ain't I? I got you now, you safe. What's your curfew?"

"I'm Twenty Six, I don't have a curfew. "

"Good, take a ride with me. Call yo' people and let them know you with me so they don't be worried about you."

"Oh, so being with you automatically make me safe?" She asked him, throwing her head to the side.

"Baby girl," he responded, raising the black nine millimeter in the air. Mystic jumped at the size of the glock, noticing that it wasn't the same pistol Spider was carrying earlier that day.

"Ain't nothin' gon' happen to you when you with me, you hear me. These cats over here don't want none of this. Trust me, you safe."

"Exactly how many of those things do you have. That ain't the same one..."

"No Questions Ma," He interrupted. "One of my nigga's needed my other one to handle some business."

Mystic's question reminded Spider to call Perez and make sure he had gotten rid of the guns they had used earlier to smoke them nigga's on Sherry.

Spider turned off Union onto Natural Bridge and rode down towards Fairgrounds Park, bumping Keith Sweat's, **Telling Me No Again.**

The bass mesmerized Mystic and she fell hook-line-and-sinker, into the whole feel of things. She smiled as Spider sung the words of the song to her in an animated version.

"*...there you go telling me know again, there u go, there u go. I wanna be more than just your friend, don't you know, don't you know. Need to be mine, girl don't you want me baby? Cause I really, really, really wanna be yours, all to myself..*"

As the Suburban came to a stop and hooked a right on Newstead Avenue, Mystic watched as Spider handled his business with a light skinned, good haired, stocky fellow. She felt a little awkward being with him while conducted his business but she relaxed as she tried to think of it as being no different than when Spider would come across the block to serve her sister Punkin.

When he got back in the truck, he looked to her and asked, "You uncomfortable with this?"

She wasn't truthfully, but not enough to admit it to him. Mystic didn't want Spider to think that she wasn't strong enough to handle the street life. She knew that thugs wanted a woman who could handle their own and have their back when needed. She wanted to be that woman for Spider. Anything she had to learn, she would learn as they went along.

"Naw, it doesn't bother me at all. I like the way you get out here and do yo' thang. Like the way you carry your weight."

Spider snickered and smiled.

"You do huh," he said putting the truck in gear.

"That's good, cause like I told you earlier, you gon' be mines."

Spider drove West on Natural Bridge Blvd. to Shreve Ave and hit Hwy 70 East towards downtown.

"I wanna show you somethin'."

His hip started to vibrate again and his face tensed up as he read the incoming caller's name.

"Something wrong," Mystic asked him, noticing the look on his face.

"I gotta take of something, hang on."

Spider exited the Hwy 70, at the downtown 10th Street exit, went down to Cass Ave., made a left, went to 9th St., and made a left to head West, back towards the hood. He was now talking to the caller on the phone. He was getting more upset by the second and Mystic had the gut feeling, he was talking to a woman.

She just sat back and stared out the window until he finished his conversation. By the time he had hung up the phone, he was pulling up in front of Mystic's house. Her feelings were a little hurt that their night had to come to an end so soon, especially after she waited so long to see him but her heart lightened as he placed his hand on her thigh and told her he'd be right back.

Chapter Six

Right back turned into a knock on her basement window on the side of the house, at two am. Mystic pulled on her jeans and headed upstairs for the door. When she opened it, she almost fainted. Spider was covered in blood. He had blood all over his t-shirt for the second time that day. He also had blood on his shorts and hands.

Mystic didn't know how to respond to his request to come inside. Spider had this look on his face that reached out to her, said he needed her and her heart responded.

Mystic open the door and led him by the hand through the front room and straight to the bathroom. She placed her hand to her mouth, gesturing him to stay quiet and then she reached over and closed her sister Punkin's bedroom door.

Mystic closed the bathroom door, turned on the shower and stood in front of Spider. No words were passed between them. She looked into his eyes and reached up to touch his face. Gliding her hands down to his waist and underneath his blood soaked t-shirt. She pulled his t-shirt over his head and threw it onto the floor. She stared at his chest and her mouth watered. Mystic was so captivated by him.

She unbuckled his black leather belt and unsnapped his blue jean shorts. She unzipped his pants as her heart began to race uncontrollably. The thought of seeing his dick with her own eyes, had the muscles in her mommy going into overdrive.

Mystic slid her fingers inside the elastic band of his jockey briefs and pulled both his briefs and shorts down to his ankles. As Spider stepped out of his clothing, he stared at Mystic and felt a strange type of connection to her.

He didn't fight it. Something about her had his attention. Something, he didn't want to let go of, despite the fact that he was married. He thought about telling her, it just wasn't the right

43

moment, not that moment. At that moment, he was too busy enjoying the way she was taking care of him.

She slowly began peeling off her top, exposing her pink lace bra with her size 36 breasts, filling out the cups, so fully. She reached around her back and un-latched her bra, letting it fall down onto the floor. Spider didn't budge; he just stared at her, amazed at how beautiful she was to him.

His heart too, began to race as he watched Mystic unbutton her jeans and lowered them down her thighs along with her pink lace panties.

She reached behind her, into the cabinet and grabbed two wash towels and two fluffy bath towels. She grabbed Spider by the hand, pulled back the black shower curtain and guided him into the awaiting steamy shower. The water was so hot as Mystic stood with her back to Spider, feeling his body so close to her, made her nipples erect.

She lathered the wash cloth with Ocean Breeze scented body wash and turned to him. She made eye contact as she placed the towel softly against his chest and began to wash the blood from his skin. Mystic washed his chest, his arms, his shoulders, his hands and his thighs. She tried so hard to avoid brushing across his jimmy but it wasn't easy. It was rock hard and standing at attention. It was so big to her, so smooth and defiant.

She re-lathered her towel and gently wrapped it around his jimmy. Her pussy jumped, it tingled and her legs were getting weak the more she touched it. She squeezed it and turned her wrist to massage it as she stroked it to clean it.

Spider ran his hands down her shoulders and continued down to her waist.

"Damn I'm feeling you."

Mystic smiled and answered as she looked down at his jimmy, "Umm, I'm feeling you too."

Then she quickly pulled back. She didn't want him to think she was easy and cheap. She wanted to be special to him, wanted him to be as crazy about her as she was about him. Mystic instructed him to turn around so she could wash his back. It felt so strong, like he could carry the weight of the world on his shoulders.

Spider turned around and Mystic looked into his eyes.

"Don't you wanna know what happened?"

Mystic shook her head "no." Apart of her was afraid to know and apart of her didn't care as long as he was the one still standing.

"I'm sure you had a good reason for whatever happened."

Mystic turned off the shower and reached outside of the curtain over to sink and grabbed one of the towels for Spider. Then she stepped out of the tub, wrapped a towel around herself and bent down to pick up all their clothing.

"Wait here."

Mystic went into the basement, back into the back closet and began digging in a box of clothing that her sister Punkin's boyfriend had left behind. She pulled out a pair of black basketball shorts and a white tee.

Mystic went into her bedroom pulled his clothes apart and removed his briefs. She gathered his blood stained clothes and threw them into the washer. Then she returned to the bathroom and handed him the clean pair of clothes and his briefs.

"Damn, you doin' it like that?" he asked her. Looking at the male clothing in his hand.

"Punkin put her boyfriend out a few weeks back and he left these behind. I put your clothes in the wash."

She pulled the wash cloth from the top of the shower rod and wrapped the gun inside. Spider watched her in amazement, she was unbelievable to him. Mystic was smart enough not to touch his gun with her bare hands. Spider found that cute.

They retired to her room as Mystic once again led Spider by the hand downstairs to the basement. Mystic's mid-sized room was decorated with African pictures, mirrors and plants. Her queen sized bed had Burgundy satin sheets and matching curtains. Her dresser, full with perfumes, oils, nail polish and sunglasses. She was a very feminine woman who loved to take care of herself.

Spider looked around and smiled to himself. He liked the way she was living. Her swagger was unique to him. Everything nice, neat and perfectly lined together.

Mystic offered Spider a seat on the bed and sat down next to him. The satin sheets felt so soft against his skin. Spider was used to the rougher side of life.

He grew up an only child in one of the roughest projects in the city of St. Louis, causing him to grow up early and quickly. It was in the JVL Projects, that Spider hooked up with his crew, Perez, Des, Kay Kay, Tank and Get Down.

Together they rose to the top in both the dope game and gangsta status in the hood. Slangin', mobbin', robbin' and killin' became apart of their everyday life. The notorious crew became known around the city as one you didn't want to mess with, not unless you could really bring the noise.

Spider had become addicted to the fast life. The money, the cars, the groupies and all the power it brought along with it, had turned him into a force to be reckoned with.

He grinded all day and played all night, bedding a different woman almost every night. He played on the way his hood status made the women so excited to be with him and he used them for what they were worth, sex and sex alone. He knew it wasn't really *him* they wanted; it was all about his money. But Spider honestly felt something different from Mystic. He didn't see her like all the others...and she wasn't.

Mystic simply wanted to be near him. Something about him made her feel stronger. As if he was the missing piece to the crazy and traumatic puzzle she called her life.

Mystic sat down on the bed beside Spider and tried to keep her stomach from doing somersaults. She wanted so badly to seduce him with everything inside her but she resisted. She didn't want him to think she was easy like most of the women he encountered. The muscles inside her mommy told her to go for it but the fear of his rejection paralyzed her and she couldn't move. Then it happened...

Spider placed his hand on her thighs just as he had done earlier in the truck and asked her, "What's on yo' mind lil' momma? You afraid of what you saw tonight?"

"Naw, I've seen more in my life than you would believe," Mystic answered, staring into his eyes.

Mystic was sure she could see the same want and the same need she felt for him, present in his eyes. She knew that if she played the "shy role" that it would only make him want her more, she was right.

Spider wanted her, just as much as she wanted him but he decided he wouldn't be the one to make the first move. He didn't want Mystic to think that he was just another dog ass nigga, trying to get between her legs, even though he had his share of women.

He wanted this one to be crazy about him, maybe even love him. Partly because she was a new commodity on the block and all his homeboys was trying to get at her. The other reason was he felt something different from her. She seemed untainted by the streets, innocent and naive almost and Spider definitely liked that in her.

He knew she wanted him but he also knew she was afraid of him. Spider had seen it in her eyes all that day. He wanted Mystic to go for what she wanted. Take the initiative to fuck him.

You could cut through the tension between them with a knife and Mystic's mommy began to throb as Spider continued to massage her thigh.

Mystic tossed around the explicit thoughts inside her head until she could no longer take it. It had been almost eight years since she'd felt a man inside of her. She'd learned to live without the hardness of a man in prison. It didn't bother her much because at the age of twenty six and inside the third year of post-divorce, Mystic had yet to experience an orgasm with a man. The only time she felt that heavenly sensation was at the hands of a woman in prison.

Mystic wanted to know what it felt like to have that explosive feeling at the hands of a real man, a thug. Beat upon her flesh until her body responded with a pulsating, orgasmic spasm.

She knew she had come to the right place because she had never felt her mommy beat like a bass drum just at the touch of a man's hand.

She decided to go for it.

If I'm gon' fuck 'em, I'm gon fuck him like he never been fucked before.

Mystic rose from the bed and walked over to the dresser. She grabbed the lotion and placed it on the bed beside Spider. Mystic opened the bottom dresser drawer and pulled out two, Cucumber Melon scented candles. She turned the desktop radio on to the Quiet Storm on Foxy 95.5 and lit the candles.

Mystic kept her eyes off of Spider the entire time but she knew he was watching her. She sucked her stomach in and tried to make her body appear sexy to him from every angle.

She dimmed the lights, walked over to the bed, reached for Spider's hand and asked him to stand.

Mystic swallowed the lump in her throat as she once again removed Spider's shorts. As she pulled the string a loose from around his waist, she followed the shorts down to his ankles, lifted his feet through to remove them; brushing against his hardness with her cheek. Her mouth water once again and she wanted to grip his jimmy inside her jaws and suck the skin off the motherfucker but Mystic calculated her every move. She was determined to blow his mind.

Spider lay down and stretched out on the bed after Mystic pulled back the satin comforter. She requested for him to lie down on his stomach so she could massage his back.

Spider smiled to himself. *See, that's the shit I'm talkin' about."*

Mystic warmed the lotion inside her hands and began down at his lower calves. She gripped his legs and worked her fingers slowly but firmly against his skin. She worked up and down, right to left, across his legs. She rubbed his inner thighs, trying to relax his muscles with the same intensity she felt boiling between her own thighs.

She slid her panties down her thighs and straddled his back, bringing her mommy to rest at the crease of his ass. She was so wet, Spider could feel her juices rolling down his butt cheeks. It was so hot against his flesh and Spider's hardness kept growing until he thought he was going to burst.

The erotic sounds of Mint Condition serenaded the moment, *"...pretty brown eyes, you know I see you. It's a disguise the way you treat me. Listen to love, your heart is pounding with desire..."*

Mystic warmed more lotion and began to massage Spider's back and his shoulders. She kneaded the crease of his spine with her knuckles and his moans let Mystic know that she was pleasing him.

She leaned down and began placing soft kisses on his neck and shoulders. She parted her lips to greet his hot flesh with her moist tongue. As she nibbled on his sides, she felt his body jerk and she chuckled.

He lay there, absorbing in the softness of her touch and her kiss. He was hard core and the way she had him feeling was so vulnerable to him. He felt a weakness for her and that was a new feeling for Spider.

Mystic continued to massage his back, his shoulders and his arms.

"You like that?" she asked him.

Spider moaned out the sweetest moan.

"Damn right."

That comment made Mystic feel both confident and super sexy.

"Turn over."

Spider followed her command as he turned over, exposing a hard-ness that made Mystic silently gasp for breath. She grabbed the lotion and began to massage his chest while staring into his eyes.

The intimidation for the moment, was gone and Mystic fell deep into his gazes. She liked the way he looked at her, as if he were telling himself, he was about to break her back.

Spider reached up and grabbed her gently by the face and pulled her down to him. Mystic's stomach quivered as his lips met hers. Spider parted his lips and began to kiss her so rough, yet she felt the passion in his kiss.

Her mommy began to pulsate once again as she gave into the longings of her heart for him. She traced the outer rim of his lips with her tongue and Spider responded by biting her bottom lip.

His hardness, pressed up against her clit, made her shiver inside and she wanted to explore it.

Mystic moved down to his chest and began to tease his nipples with her moist tongue. She had a hunger for him and she wasn't about to waist one moment worrying about what the next day might bring them.

She slid down his waist and at last, she had found her treasure. The pretty shades of colors, dancing in her eyes against the flicker of the candle light. She placed a kiss a top of it and began to lick across his thighs.

Spider let out a sigh and gripped Mystic's upper arms. She wanted to hear him scream. She picked up his jimmy and wet her tongue before gliding it across the tip of his shaft. Her tongue ring rolled across the blood vessel underneath the head.

She had her mind set on hearing him holler and as she slid her tongue down the center and wrapped her lips around his jimmy, she let the heat from her jaws sweep across his flesh. Her mouth was so warm and wet to him.

He lay there, gripping the sheets as she took his jimmy to the back of her throat and allowed it to tickle her tonsils. He could feel the tip of his jimmy pop against the hard gristle in her throat. Mystic allowed her mouth to fill with wetness as she rotated her neck and went to work on his jimmy with a hunger.

She lifted his jimmy to the side and ran her moist tongue down to his nuts. She placed one inside her mouth and began to hum a sweet melody. His body jerked, she smiled. Stroking his jimmy with her hand and swishing the juices in her mouth across the sensitive spots on his nuts. She felt his legs began to tighten.

Spider pleaded for her to stop which made her want him even more. The power she felt turned her on and she placed his jimmy back inside her mouth and went to work. She wanted to bring him to the point of climax and leave him there. Drive him insane.

Spider gripped her arms and attempted to pull her close to him but Mystic wouldn't let go of the death grip her jaws had on his jimmy. Spider felt his temperature rise and Mystic felt his hardness increase. He was near eruption.

Mystic released his jimmy and began to kiss his inner thigh.

"Turn over. I wanna rub your back again."

Spider just laid there, his heart pounding, his body sweating...his jimmy throbbing. He rolled over and Mystic began to kiss his back. Biting and teasing his skin with her tongue. She continued down to his lower back and when she reached his butt, she stuck her tongue out to greet it and continued across each cheek.

She felt his leg muscles tightened and he moaned out freely and carelessly.

"Shit mommy, what you doin' to me?"

She didn't respond. She continued her quest to be the best he ever had. Mystic spread apart his cheeks and slid her tongue between the creases of his butt. He squirmed as she twirled her tongue inside his ass and blew a cool breath across the hole.

"Un-un, stop, I can't take no more. Come here."

He used his strength to roll her over and pin her down onto the bed.

"What you trying to do, make me love you?"

Mystic stretched her neck up and kissed him with a passion, money couldn't buy. Then she reached down between his legs and rubbed the tip of his jimmy against her clit. She was on fire. She wanted this nigga, more than anything in the world. She wanted to feel him, thrusting and pounding inside her flesh. Mystic guided his jimmy inside the mound of wet juices and instantly moaned as her walls began to grip his jimmy.

Spider stared down at her. The way she bit her lip when he plunged down deep inside her, turned him on tremendously. The frown she wore when he dipped his body to the right, then back to the left; as if to touch every corner of her walls.

She raised her head to watch his body work and the visual stimulation brought her the feeling she had been searching for....she felt her body tighten, her legs locked, her breath heightened and her nails dug in for dear life.

As Jamie Foxx's *Infatuation* pumped out over the airwaves, Mystic let her juices flow. She screamed out in a passionate voice and braced herself for the explosion.

"...is it just infatuation or it real love, real love? Is it just infatuation. I have waited for so long to hear you say, I wanna spend my whole life with you. Well I don't mean to fuss, don't mean to push, I know you're all alone but there's just one thing I have to know... is it just infatuation..."

Her eyes glistened against the candle light and Spider felt the river flow upon his jimmy, down upon his nuts. He looked down at her, leaned in close and his heart melted when he saw the tears rolling down the sides of her face. He plunged deeper, wanting her to need him, wanting her to bleed him, needing her to love him.

"Is this mines, can I have this all to myself?"

Mystic shook her head.

"Look at me. I want this. I don't want no other man to feel what I'm feelin' right now. You hear me?"

Bam.

"Do you hear me?"

Bam.

"I hear you."

Bam.

"No, I wanna hear you say it."

Bam... bam... bam... bam.

"Say it."

"It's yours. It's yours, Spider, nobody will ever feel this."

Bam, bam... BOOOOOOMMM!

They came together, hard and strong. Screaming out together in ecstasy and loving every second of it. Spider collapsed on top on her, panting and out of breath.

Mystic wrapped her arms around him and held him as tightly as she could.

"Stay with me. Stay the night with me."

Spider thought of his obligations for a minute but as he looked up at her and kissed her on her lips, he didn't care about going home. Right there, in her arms was the only place he wanted to be.

Chapter Seven

Cocamo picked up the small white piece of paper lying on the front room table and stared at it's contents, "Call Me, Tee-Tee, 809-3587, Don't cheat yo'self, instead, treat yo' self."

Cocamo smirked at the comment and hit his blunt.

This bitch is crazy.

He turned the television to BET and snickered as BET Uncut videos showed 2Pac's , "*How Do You Want It.*" As Cocamo blew his head back and watched as *JoJo* from *Jodeci*, ran a golden shower down some groupie's chest, he found himself picking up the small piece of paper again.

It had been three days since he'd said a word to her, although he did see her on the block within that time frame. For Cocamo, to acknowledge her in any way after he slept with her, would be like admitting to her that she was different from all the others. He wasn't ready to play that card yet.

But he was in the mood for some company and admit it or not, she was the best thing going. He dialed the number and chuckled at the call tone. Adina Howards', "*T-shirt and Panties*" played in his ear.

When Tee-Tee saw the number come across her screen, she too let out a chuckle.

"Now this nigga wanna call a bitch after three muthafuckin' days. He a hot fuckin' mess."

She flipped open the phone and answered as if she didn't know who it was on the other end of the phone.

"Yeah?"

"Where you at, come fuck wit' me."

"Who is this?" she asked.

55

"Don't stunt, you know who the fuck this is. You comin' or not?"

"I gotta make a lil' mo' money first. Then I can come holla at you, it shouldn't take me that long."

"Naw, do you then, I'll call somebody else. I don't wait on pussy, pussy waits on me, hand-n-foot. I'll holla."

Cocamo clicked the phone and lit up his blunt. He knew the phone would ring back within ten minutes. He was right.

Tee-Tee thought about Big Slug. The way he'd been on her head to push things with Cocamo over the last couple of days and he was constantly reassuring her that as long as Cocamo was stealing his business that she too wouldn't be able to eat out in the streets too much longer.

The fact that Cocamo called her, kind of touched her. Tee-Tee knew he had plenty of other options but he chose her, which in a strange way, meant something. So, she hit the *send* button on her Samsung-flip phone to call him back.

"Aight, give me about ten minutes, that cool?"

"Nine."

Click.

Cocamo hung up the phone, rolled two blunts and laid them on the table. He took out his ½ pint of Patron and Cranberry juice and made him a drink. He wanted to get his bladder full. He had plans for her.

When Tee-Tee knocked on the door, Cocamo stepped aside to let her in.

"I thought you'd change yo' mind. You know you want this good. I don't even know why you was tryin' to stunt. Must've been around them lil' bitch ass nigga's you run wit'. Betta check yo'self girl, I'm that nigga."

"Whatever Nigga, you got some heat?"

"Always, it's on the table, gon' fire up."

Get nice and good cause I'm finna fuck the dog shit out yo' ass, he said to himself, smirking as he went into the kitchen to get her a glass.

"You on that 'Tron with me?"

"I guess so shit, last time that shit had me dozin' off."

"It ain't gon' be that strong this time. A nigga ain't call you over here to watch you slob and shit, not on no pillow anyway," he chuckled.

"Very funny, muthafucka."

Cocamo poured her a drink, headed back into the living room and sat down next to Tee-Tee. He sat the drink down in front of her and took the blunt from her hand. He inhaled the chronic and began to cough.

"That nigga Spider came through again. This shit is fire."

"Ain't it though," Tee-Tee agreed.

Cocamo cut up the TV to increase the sounds to his favorite *Bun B* video.

"...You want money and jewels, you want clothes and cars, wanna live VIP, rubbin' shoulder wit stars. Wanna fly in G4's or sail the seas, then your wish is my command. If you need love, I'm lovin'. If you need a thug, I'm thuggin'. If you need a hustla'... whatever you need, girl I'm a hold you down..."

"That's that raw shit right there. That nigga came hard as a muthafucka on this shit," Cocamo said, bobbin' his head to the beat.

"That shit is just entertainment. Nigga's out here ain't really holdin' it down like that. Out in these streets, its' get what you can get and get a muthafucka befo' they get you. The game done change since our parents was kickin' it. Ain't no real love in the world no more.

Now days, nigga's just wanna lay up in yo' shit, scratch they asses, eat up yo' food and don't wanna help you do shit. Ask a muthafucka fo' some money on the rent or bills and they get ghost."

"Damn, you sound a lil bitter baby, you need a hug or somethin'," Cocamo said, chuckling.

Tee-Tee hit Cocamo on the arm.

"Fuck you nigga, I'm serious. Just think about it fo' a minute. Don't nobody make love no mo', all a nigga say he wanna do, is break yo' back out."

Cocamo snickered and gave her a Mr. Grinch type smile.

"Shit, you know it," he said, inhaling the blunt.

"See that's what I'm talkin' about. Why it gotta be like that? Whatever happen to havin' a down ass chick on yo' arm? That's the type of shit I wanna be on, some of that Bonnie and Clyde shit. I want a nigga who gon' have my back the same way I'm gon' have his. What's wrong with that?"

"What's wrong with it? What's right with it? This ain't that type of game out here no mo'. You just said yo'self, everybody is out fo' themselves. Bitches now days done took gold diggin' to a whole new level. They fuck you, yo' patna's, yo' daddy and anybody you know, to get that doe in they pockets. The problem ain't the nigga's, it's the bitches. The bitches done crossed so many of these nigga's out here, settin' 'em up and shit, that now the nigga's done took the game and gone with it."

"That's bullshit."

"Is it? We learned the game from ya'll. We come straight out a bitches' womb. How many nigga's you know are sittin' in the pen right now from a bitch that got mad and called them boys on his ass cause he smacked the hoe once or twice? Bitches is scandalous. If it don't benefit 'em or if it's a threat that it might stop benefittin' 'em, they twist the game and do some bunk shit like set his ass up or somethin'."

Tee-Tee leaned back on the couch and exhaled. She thought about the reason she was tryin' to get up close and personal with Cocamo. It was for profit.

Damn, am I like that fo' real?

Cocamo put the blunt out and leaned back next to her on the couch.

"I mean, you here fo' the same reason ain't you?"

Tee-Tee's stomach quivered and her breath got caught in her throat.

Does he know somethin's up? Is that why he really called me over here?

"What you mean by that?" she asked him.

"I mean, you ain't over here cause you straight dig a nigga or nothin', you over here cause you want that good shoved up in you. Right or wrong?"

"Fuck you, nigga."

"That's exactly what I'm talkin' about. That's what you came here fo'."

There was a knock on the door. Cocamo rose up from the couch and walked over to the door. He peeped out the window at the scraggly looking fiend and told him to go around to the back of the house. When Tee-Tee heard the fiend's voice, it sounded all too familiar. She knew it well... RJ.

Cocamo turned to Tee-Tee, told her he'd be right back and left the room. When she saw him head towards the back door off the kitchen, she tip-toed to the hallway and tried to overhear his conversation with RJ.

"Nigga, you know betta than to knock on my muthafuckin' front door. You never know whose up in this piece. It's a muthafuckin' war goin' on right now and you crooked teeth muthafucka's is the bait."

Tee-Tee couldn't hear RJ's response but it really didn't matter either way. She now knew Cocamo was doing exactly what Big Slug accused him of doing, purposely stealing their customers. She hurried back to the couch and resumed her position as she heard the back door close. When he returned to the front room, she asked if she could use the bathroom. Once inside the bathroom, Tee-Tee pulled out her phone from her pocket and began texting Big Slug.

"... *u right, I just got proof he's sellin' 2 our people. RJ just left frm ovr here coppin' frm him...*"

As Cocamo went into his room to add his proceeds to his stash, Big Slug, texted back.

"... *I fuckin' knew that part already Sherlock, y the fuck u think u there? Handle that...*"

When Tee-Tee walked back into the front room, she sat back down next to Cocamo, took a swig of her Patron and leaned back. She was getting buzzed quickly. She looked over at Cocamo. She didn't want to get into a conversation with him concerning Big Slug's business but on the other hand, Big Slug's words rang in her ear.

The more of our business he takes, the less you eat out here on these streets.

"So ummm, you been in the game fo' a minute, right? Cause I was just sittin' here and I'm really wonderin', what part of the game was that?"

"Was what?"

"I know that nigga RJ's voice from anywhere... what's up with you servin' our folks?"

"Shit, cash rules everything 'round me. You don't see me standin' on no muthafuckin' corners, do you? I don't go out searchin' fo' dope fiends. They knock on my muthafuckin' door. And if that nigga Big Slug stop sellin' that bullshit he got, he wouldn't be loosin' his folks. Everybody knows that nigga ain't had no good dope in months. Cuttin' that shit down so he can make mo' profit. Nigga's highs ain't lastin' but three seconds to a muthafuckin' minute. Them the complaints I get."

Tee-Tee pulled her purse closer to her. She didn't know which bag Cocamo was about to come out of but she wanted to be prepared. Yet, within seconds, he clamed his demeanor and took his seat back beside her.

"Look, I didn't call you over here for all that. You down or what? Cause I ain't finna spend my night talkin' bout no wack ass nigga like Big Slug."

Tee-Tee looked at the Patron on the table and then to the bulge that was beginning to form down Cocamo's thigh. She took another sip of her drink, handed the empty glass to him for a refill and smirked.

"I'm down."

Cocamo rose up from the couch and sneered at her.

"I thought you would be."

Chapter Eight

Mystic sat out on the steps, enjoying the beautiful weather and waiting on the tan Suburban to hit the corner. She hadn't heard from him since he'd left at the crack of dawn that morning. Actually, she was a little worried about him. It was unlike him for all his boys to be out on the block but not him.

He loved the grind to much to miss out on making money. Mystic thought back to the night before. The way he looked at her when she opened the door for him. All the blood covering his shirt and shorts.

She felt so important being able to help him, illegal and all she didn't care. All she knew was that his eyes were calling out her and couldn't resist answering. She understood the risk in getting involved with him. She knew his lifestyle and she also knew it could be damaging to her freedom. But for some strange reason, it excited her. His need for her gave her a feeling she hadn't felt in a long time, special.

She removed her cell phone from her waist, flipped it open, smiled at the wallpaper of her baby girl's picture and then searched her phone book for his number. Mid-dial, the Suburban pulled up to the corner, bumping the sounds of R-Kelly's, Seems Like You're Ready.

"...temperatures rising and your body's yearnin' for me. Girl lay it on me, I'll place no one above thee, oh, take me to your ecstasy. It seems like your read, girl are you ready, to go all the way..."

Mystic closed her eyes and for a moment, relived the previous night. Her clit jumping at the thought of how he gently brushed his tongue across its flesh and the way he wrapped his lips around it and slightly pulled on it with his jaws.

The sight of him made her mouth water. But her thoughts were interrupted by the sound of her sister Breeze's voice, who was now sitting behind her on the porch.

"That fucka is such a fuckin' bastard. I called his ass two hours ago fo' a sac."

Rhonda A.K.A. Breeze, was Mystic's next oldest sister. She was a thicker version of Mystic with short cropped coal black hair. Breeze, unlike most girls in the hood didn't have to work if she didn't want to. Everything she wanted was handed to her on a silver platter thanks to her boyfriend, Man, who only fucked with the big boys in the hood.

Standing at five-foot two, dark skin, braids and fang style gold's, Man was also sexy to the women in the neighborhood. He had an arrogance about himself that often intimidated most women in his presence but you couldn't help but be attracted to it. He changed women, like he changed his clothes. Why not? Being one of the major players in the hood, other than Big Slug, brought him great wealth, along with the ability to splurge on both, whatever and whomever.

Man didn't dazzle in bullshit, he moved real weight and if you weren't talkin' about spending more than chump change with him, he would simply tell you, *"let your back get smaller,"* meaning, turn around and keep it moving.

Breeze, while a pretty girl herself, often wondered what Man saw in her. Man in her eyes, as in most women's eyes, could have any woman he wanted.

Breeze often joked around, that fucking with Man could both, hypnotize you and mesmerize you. Thus, making her get into some crazy shit, to hold on to him. Breeze often rode the Greyhound Bus to Virginia, to pick up his packages and bring it back to the Lou. Holding his product whenever they bent corners together, just in case the law pulled them over, she could easily stash it inside her vagina. Breeze often wore short skirts for that purpose… easy access, both for him or his dope, whichever he preferred.

Breeze often figured that with her taking the bigger risks, it would keep her, getting broke off the biggest piece of the pie… she was right. Man kept her laced in the finest of gear, begets and a pocket full of money. The only thing he didn't do, was supply her *Chronic* habit, which was the reason she was now sitting on the porch, letting Spider have it.

"He had a long night," Mystic blushed.

"So, I heard," Breeze responded, putting fire to the tip of her last, half of blunt.

"I heard yawl's nasty asses in there. Bitch couldn't even get no sleep."

"My bad," Mystic said, hitting her on the bottom of her leg.

Breeze leaned down and offered Mystic the blunt.

"Bitch, you know I'm on probation, I can't fuck with that."

"Right, I forgot. So how was it," Breeze asked, being nosey.

"What?"

"The dick, bitch, how was the dick?"

Mystic smiled.

"Girl, it was the bomb!" she stated, excitedly. "That nigga got that good. He handled his business but I handled mines, too. He cold at …"

"Hol' up," Breeze interrupted, putting her finger up to her lips. "Here he comes."

Mystic watched as he walked across the street. The way he walked had new meaning to her since she now knew what was up underneath his baggy shorts and all she could do is smile.

"What it do, mommy? What's good?"

"You," Mystic replied.

"Fuck all that mushy shit, you bastard. Where's my dub I called you fo' two fuckin' hours ago?" Breeze cut in.

"My bad Breeze, I got you. Them boys tried to helm me up round the corner."

"Whatever nigga., you just slow, muthafucka."

"Naw, fo' real Breeze, I bullshit you not. They came at me wit' some shit 'bout some nigga that got popped last night on Acme."

He looked to Mystic and winked his eye.

"Well, you here now and I think, I should get compensation fo' all my pain and suffering from waitin' on yo' ass."

Spider reached down inside his shorts and pulled out his bag of medicine. He in fact, gave her an extra dub-sac, for waiting on him and not taking her business elsewhere. Spider loved that loyalty in his clients.

As Breeze held the chronic to her nostrils to inhale its contents, she saw the black, Jeep Wrangler pull up in front of the house. A smile as wide as the Mississippi came across her face.

Man emerged from the driver's side of the jeep, dressed in dark blue Phem shorts and a red and white, Cardinals jersey. He had on some fresh red and white Nike shoes and his red STL ball cap. Mystic shook her head and looked to Breeze.

Damn, that muthafucka know his ass is fine! Mystic thought to herself. *Ump, ump ump!*

Man threw up two fingers to his homeboys down the street, then proceeded to walk up the steps. He playfully hit Mystic on the bottom of her leg and then gave Spider some dap.

He looked up onto the porch at Breeze and gestured for her to come to him with a quick throw back of his head.

"I need you to take a ride with me over by the Chain-of Rocks. I need to clear my head fo' a minute, befo' I go *lo-co* on these muthafucka's. Somebody popped my lil cousin on Acme last night as he was leaving Club Legit."

"Marco?" Breeze asked.

"Yeah, they say he got into some static in the club with some nigga's from the west side but it was a northside nigga rollin' with 'em that caught him round the corner. So, I'm tryin' to get my head together befo' I start a war out here, you feel me?"

Mystic noticed Spider staring off at the ground as Man talked about his cousin being shot. Then she thought back to the night before. She never asked him, partly because she didn't think she could handle the answer. But looking at his face as Man spoke, she knew. Either he did it or he knew who did it.

"Aey man, lets go get somethin' to drink on," Man told Spider.

Spider looked to Mystic.

"Come on Mommy, let's ride."

Man, Breeze, Spider and Mystic jumped into Man's jeep and headed down Mimika to West Florissant. Man pulled into the F&G Liquor Store on Riverview and West Florissant to grab a half-pint of Remy. It helped him think when he needed to. When he got to the counter, he tipped his favorite cashier, Gloria, clowned around with his patna' Tony, who had a slight limp but was cool with everybody in the neighborhood, exchanged words with Cookie and headed outside.

When Spider and Man reached the door, Lil Curtis called out to him.

"Aey, Aey… Man, I gotta holla at you man."

Lil Curtis, dressed in a pink bathrobe, a pair of tube socks pulled up to his knees (that led to a pair of the ashiest knees you could imagine), a pair of boxers and a wife beater, both looked and sounded just like *Ezelle* from *Friday* . It was always so hard to take him serious because he was always clowning around.

Despite his hilarious attire, Man sensed a serious tone in his voice.

"What up?" Man responded.

"It's bout yo' cuz, Man. Nigga's is talkin' alot round these streets, like 'er body plottin' to be yo' next right hand man and shit. Like I tell these nigga's, if it be anybody, it'll be me," he said popping the collar on his fuzzy robe.

"Dig, cause can't nobody out here do this shit like me, you hear me?"

Man chuckled at the silliness in his voice and gave him a few dollars to grab him a beer.

"Aight then, I'm out." Man told him, turning to walk away.

"Cause see man," Lil Curtis continued, as he followed Man to the truck. "I'm so cold, I can sell a tank of gas to the muthafuckin' gas company, a bucket of water to the fire hydrant.

Nigga, I'm so smooth, I can sell a case of Slim Fast to a bitch that's anorexic."

Man chuckled and opened the door to his truck. He was glad he'd run into Lil Curtis. He needed a good laugh but he was also thankful for the information. He knew nigga's was gon' come at him but he didn't think it would be this soon.

Lil Curtis waved at Breeze and Mystic in the jeep.

"What's up, ladies?"

Breeze and Mystic smiled and returned his wave.

"Aey but fo' real Man, quit playin'. Put me on, nigga. I make shit happen."

With that, he looked over the top of Man's truck, side to side, snatched his robe closed in a "Sweet Daddy from Good Times" swing and nodded a quick nod.

"Gone! Like a like dick between a fat bitch's thighs!"

Man put the truck in gear and bagged out the parking spot. As he fumbled with the system in his car they could hear Lil' Curtis in the distance, yelling to Cocamo. Cocamo and Spider made eye contact and threw up the peace sign to each other.

"Aey... Aey Cocamo, let me holla at you." Lil Curtis yelled to Cocamo.

Man just shook his head and laughed.

"That's one stupid ass boy," he told Breeze as she chuckled in agreement. Man popped the top on his Remy and took a swig. Breeze could tell his mind was deep in thought on his little cousin. She just rode along side him but didn't say anything. One thing she learned in dealing with Man was he was not the kind of guy you wanted to press or bag into a corner.

You couldn't force him to talk, let alone express his feelings or emotions. Being raised in the streets, meant he was always on guard with everybody, especially women. He had watched a lot of his homies end up behind the walls from fucking with scandalous bitches. Women that had gotten pissed off because they got played and ended up set them up to get robbed. Put in jail or some killed. Man was aware of the fact that most hoes in the streets would rather see you locked up, than with another woman. So he kept his thoughts and his business for the most part to himself.

He simply didn't trust women. Yet, after alot of tests and bullshit, he had come to trust Breeze. She had earned his heart through the grind. Man respected the hustle in her, plus the fact that she would do any and everything he wanted her to do, at the drop of a dime.

Spider didn't talk much on the way to, or from the store. Mystic knew that meant he was feeling uncomfortable around Man. When they pulled back onto the block, Mystic excused herself and went into the house. When she returned a few minutes later, Breeze was gone and so was Man.

She sat down on the porch and thought about the severity of the situation. Not only was she getting involved with a thug while on probation but she had to ask herself, what would it do to her relationship with her sister if Breeze found out Spider may have killed Man's cousin.

Maybe I'm out of my league on this one, Mystic thought to herself. But as Spider took a seat beside her on the steps and placed a kiss on her right shoulder, that doubt quickly went away.

"I missed you today," she told him.

"I missed you too, mommy. I got caught up. But I'm here now, so it's good."

He nonchalantly, turned to look over his right shoulder and check the corner. His wife would be getting home from work any minute and she was already on his head for staying out all night.

She had seen his truck parked across the street on Harney on her way to work that morning but rather than stop and check, she just assumed he'd fallen asleep at the house where he made his money.

Spider looked back towards Mystic's front door.

"Where Punkin at?"

"She next door over Unc's house. You know she go over there everyday around this time to blow her head back and watch, *The Young and the Restless*," Mystic responded.

"Unc hittin' that?"

"I don't think so."

"Bullshit, Unc taxin' that ass. Anyway, while everybody gone, I need you to go and get that piece you hid for me last night. I need to get rid of it."

It was her opportunity to ask but Mystic resigned. She didn't want to over step her bounds. She wanted him to learn to trust her as Man trusted Breeze. To the point that he would know that he could share with her, all his dirty secrets and know in his heart, they'd stay just between the two of them. Then and only then she reasoned, would he give her the life that Man was giving to Breeze. And like Breeze, Mystic reasoned within herself that if she took the bigger risks to hold him down, she would get the bigger benefits, so she decided to try to score some major points with him.

"It's already gone, you don't have to worry about nobody in this house findin' it."

Spider looked at her confused.

"Gone, gone where?"

Mystic looked at Spider and smiled.

"I kinda figured you'd done somethin' bad last night. It was impossible for you to have all that blood on you and the other person, not be dead. Trust me, I don't wanna know what happened cause conspiracy is a muthafucka and it don't even matter to me.

But why get rid of yo' clothes and not the gun. So when I went inside a lil while ago, while Man was talkin', I went downstairs, moved the washer and threw it down the washer drain. The washer don't work, so it's safe until you have the chance to move it later, after things have calmed down."

"My mommy, I knew you had it in you. Come on let's go ridin' and maybe if we see somethin' you like, I'll buy you somethin' nice." Spider said, pulling her into his arms and placing a kiss on her cheek.

Mystic smiled to herself. She knew deep inside that the game came with risks but she was now on track to getting the life she wanted.

Chapter Nine

Cocamo admired the loyalty in Tee-Tee. Even if it was to a weak ass nigga like Big Slug. He smirked at her as he slid his hand across her thigh. Tee-Tee asked if she could use his bathroom again. When she got up, she was so buzzed, she left her purse on the couch, halfway opened.

Cocamo, always being cautious, glanced at the bathroom door to make sure it still closed, slid the purse over to himself, unsnapped it and peeked inside. He pulled out her *"infant sized"* stack of cash and chuckled.

"All that muthafuckin' loyalty fo' crumbs," he said, continuing to look from inside her purse to the bathroom door.

A slight grin lined his face as he took his pinkie finger and slid it inside the trigger slot of her black and pink pearl handled .22. He held it in the air and nodded his head.

"Aww, ain't that cute? She got a baby pistol to go with her baby hustle."

When he heard the toilet flush, he dropped the .22 back inside the purse, re-snapped it back together and slid it back across the couch. His mind began wondering why Tee-Tee stayed up under Big Slug. He wondered was Big Slug holding something over her head, other than money. He started trying to put two and two, together and he didn't really didn't care for the way things were starting to add up.

But as soon as Tee-Tee walked out of the bathroom, wearing nothing but her birthday suit, Cocamo put the math class in recess. He sat back, blunt to his lips and smiled to himself. He liked that *in* her and he knew he was about to like it *up* in her as well.

Tee-Tee was pleased with the look she saw on Cocamo's face, But her facial expressions quickly changed as soon as she noticed her purse on the couch.

"Did he look in my shit? What if this nigga saw my heat in there and took it out?

Tee-Tee had all kinds of thoughts running through her head. She slowly began to panic. She had to think quickly on her feet. She didn't get this far in the game by being dumb. She walked over to the couch, kneeled down in front of him and ran her hands down his chest. Her plan was to undress him and make sure her pistol wasn't in his waist or in his pockets.

When she reached his belt buckle, she unfastened it, never breaking eye contact with him. She watched his shoulders. Every move he could have possibly made could be determined by his shoulders. She unbuttoned his Phem jeans and unzipped his pants.

"Stand up," she told him, reassuring herself that she had to take control of the situation and of his mind.

Cocamo, although still unsure of her reasons for entering his crib with a pistol, complied with her demands. He knew that if anything popped off, that he could more than handle himself against Tee-Tee, so he put all that nonsense to the back of head and focused on the naked beauty in front of him and what he was about to do to her.

Not to get it twisted, he had every intention of finding out if she was up anything shady, just after he broke her back. Tee-Tee slid his pants and boxers down his legs. She felt a little vulnerable because of the physical position she was in; but he'd have to reach down to grab his gun and if he made that move she'd attack. Bite his jimmy clean off his body, nuts and all.

Instead, she untied his shoe laces, removed his shoes, and slid his pants and boxers over his feet. Cocamo's jimmy was so hard. He had so much anticipation, running through his body. It was good to him the last time and something told him it would be even better this time around.

He started to sit down but Tee-Tee stopped him. She wanted him to feel the power over her. Power she was allowing him to have over her for the moment. Her submission as someone he could have his way with anyway he wanted, would place her in a position to be on top later.

She bit him on his inner thighs and felt his leg quiver. She liked that. She ran her tongue up his nuts and closed her lips around the lower side of his jimmy up to the triangular tip. She swished the saliva around in her mouth to make it even moister.

She engulfed him inside her jaws with a force. She did her best to capture his mind as she turned her head side-to-side, with each stroke. Cocamo was in heaven. He liked the way she made him feel. He reached around her head and begun to gyrate his body against her head. She responded by grabbing at the back of his legs, squeezing his thighs.

Cocamo moaned and told her how good it felt.

"You on this dick, ain't you?"

In his mind, he was talking to himself as well.

Shit, if this bitch is here to kill me; fuck it, let a nigga go out like this!

He pushed her away from him and told her to stand up. He didn't no why but he no longer wanted to break her *down*, he wanted to break her *in*. He knew that with the way she was putting it down, she wasn't going anywhere no time soon. He turned her around and with her back pressed against his jimmy, Cocamo guided her back to his bedroom.

Inside, he threw Tee-Tee down on the bed, reached inside his top drawer and retrieved a Trojan. He plunged inside her, no thought of the moment after; he needed to capture her mind, so whatever hold Big Slug had on her, would soon be his. He put his hands underneath her ass and drove deeper.

"I like this pussy."

"Nigga, I like this dick," Tee-Tee replied, gripping the bed.

"You on some bullshit or did you really come cause wanted this dick."

Tee-Tee couldn't even put an answer together for that one. She was engulfed in the pleasure she felt beneath her pelvis and all she could say was, "I came for you."

Cocamo slightly chuckled and pumped harder, stronger.... deadlier. He was enjoying her, against his will, so the only way out for him was to control both the situation and her. He had made it up in his mind that he soon would control her... mind, body and soul.

Chapter Ten

When the Suburban pulled back onto the block, Mystic was riding high from the time she'd spent with Spider. They had gone to the Playboy's Bar & Grill, on Broadway to have a shrimp dinner.

Spider ordered him a shot of Crown Royal and ordered Mystic a Strawberry Daiquiri. He looked across the table at her and chuckled.

"What? Why you laughing at me?"

"I'm really trying to figure out, what yo' lil' ass could've done to go do seven years."

"*Seven and a half,*" she said, stretching her neck at him. "Don't take my half away from me. And it wasn't like I was trying to be tough or anything like that. I was defending myself."

"From?"

"Him," she responded, looking off. "I mean, he had me out there, writing checks and shit. It was as simple as "do or die.""

"Why is that?" Spider asked her.

"Because if I didn't he liked to fight."

"That nigga was beatin' on you?"

Mystic shook her head and began to explain how her life had gon' up until the point of her incarceration. The ups and the downs...downs mostly. Spider grabbed her pinkie finger with his and began to shake it.

"Don't sweat it mommy, you with me now. Ain't nobody gon' ever fuck with you, believe that. One thing I don't play about is what's mines."

He pulled her close to him.

"And you mines!"

It seemed as if the world had lifted from her shoulders with the touch of his lips. She knew at that moment, she would love him. He pulled back from her and smiled.

"Say the word, they all dead."

She liked that. Like the way it sounded... protective. They continued to chit-chat over drinks and Mystic told Spider of her dream to be a writer and poet some day.

"Maybe one day you'll write my story."

Mystic smiled.

"I don't know, are you worth writing about?"

He winked his eye at her.

"You know I am, that's why you with me."

"Then, maybe I will."

Mystic was still in a daze when the Suburban came to a halt at the stop sign of Mimika at Shulte. She didn't notice the cars at first but when the nine undercover detectives' surrounded the truck, reality soon came crashing down around her.

You could hear the shouting and commands blurring from their mouths, over his music. Spider looked to Mystic, the fright on her face, staring back at him. He told her it would be okay.

He put the truck into *park,* and held his hands up as the detective snatched open his door and yanked him out of the driver's seat. They immediately threw him down onto the ground and stepped onto his upper back until they got the cuffs on him.

Mystic watched in horror and they stood him up and placed him into the back of an awaiting unmarked car. Mystic looked at the detective standing on her side of the truck, now ordering her to exit the vehicle. The middle aged black officer placed his hand on the handle and opened the door while his side arm stayed aimed at Mystic.

She stepped out of the truck to the yelling of her sister Punkin, who came running off the porch and down the street, followed by Unc.

"What you doin' to my sister? She ain't did nothin'."

The detective looked over to Punkin and told her to bag off.

"We just trying to get the situation under control Ma'am, don't make it worse."

Unc stepped closer to him.

"Is all that shit necessary?'

"Sir, I'm not gon' tell ya'll again. You can see these cuffs to if you'd like."

"Man, I ain't scared of no damn cuffs, I did time befo', it ain't no thang to me! I just wanna watch yo' every move while you harrasin' my niece. Case I need to call, *Contact 2* and report yo' ass."

The detective shook off Unc's comments and asked Mystic for her ID. Mystic stomach tied in knots as the free officer's began to search Spider's truck.

Mystic pulled out her state ID and handed it to the officer.

"I need you to sit down on the curve with your hands behind yo' back until I run you through the computer. And don't move."

Mystic looked around at the crowd that gathered to watch the spectacle. She was embarrassed but at the same time, she felt like a hood celebrity. Get Down, Tank, Harvey, Lil Curtis, and Toi and all the crew had rushed down to check on their homeboy.

Punkin leaned in close to Mystic.

"What he do?"

"Nothin', we just came back from eatin' at Playboy's, stopped by J-Mar's and came home. They jumped out from no where."

"Well, don't say shit to they ass. You don't know nothin', you ain't heard nothin' and you ain't seen nothin', got it?"

Mystic nodded her head.

Unc added his two cents to the conversation, telling Mystic that she wasn't new to the game.

"You been down befo', you know how these muthafucka's work. They can't twist words you don't let come out yo' mouth, feel me?"

Mystic nodded her head again and looked across the street to Spider, who was now leaning up against a cruiser, talking to a detective.

They made eye contact and Mystic's heart went out to him. She knew enough to know that they were probably questioning him about the shooting last night. She also knew that without a weapon and an alibi, they couldn't touch him.

When the detective returned to Mystic, he told her to stand up but not to leave. He gave her back her ID and asked her about her Fed ID number that came up in the computer.

"I'm on probation."

"So, what you doin' with him? You didn't know he was a convicted felon?"

"No, I just met him and he asked me out. Last night was our first date."

Mystic smiled to herself. The thought of Spider doing time made her want him even more. He could understand her like no one else could.

"Well, I suggest you find yo'self a new boyfriend cause this one's on his way downtown."

Mystic looked around the officer to see them putting Spider in the back of the cruiser. Before they closed the door, he called Get Down over to the car. Get Down in turn, yelled out something to Tank, that almost made Mystic faint.

"Aey Tank, go around the corner and get his wife so she can come and get his truck."

His what? Wife? I know he did not just say his wife?

Mystic looked at Spider who could read the expression on her face and hung his head down. It was not his intention for her to find out this way.

Mystic turned to Punkin and Punkin noticed her expression as well.

"What, you ain't know?"

Mystic shook her head.

"Does it matter?" Punkin asked.

Mystic didn't respond.

"Look girl, you might as well get over that shit and quick. I mean, who the fuck ain't married? We at a shortage on nigga's out here or did you forget. They either dead, in jail or gay, so nigga's is either married, stay with they baby momma or somethin'.

Besides, he must don't give a fuck, he ain't leave here 'til the crack of dawn, right? And he just took you to eat *in* the hood, not out in St. Charles no where. So if he don't care, what the fuck is yo' problem?"

Mystic pondered her words for a minute. She was right, why should it matter to her? It didn't seem to matter to those hoes that constantly slept with her husband when she was married. If he could give her what she wanted, who cared if he sung another woman to sleep with his snoring every night?

The tall, thin detective that had ordered Spider from the truck, came across the street as the cruiser with him seated in the back, pulled off.

"Ma'am, I need to ask you a few questions."

"She ain't got no answers fo' you," Punkin chimed in.

The officer looked to Punkin and then back to Mystic.

"The easy way here or the hard way down at the station."

Mystic sat down on the step to their front porch and asked him what he wanted to know.

"Mr. Cobb's says he was with you last night. First off, is that true and secondly, if it is, from what time to what?"

Mystic thought of what Punkin said and what Breeze had, that she wanted. If Spider knew that she'd gotten him out of this one, she'd move to the top of his list.

"He picked me up from work last night. I got off at eleven and then he came here with me and he didn't leave 'til this morning around five thirty."

The officer looked at Mystic skeptically.

"You sure about that? 5:30?"

"I know how to tell time. It was five-thirty cause I looked at the clock when I got up to let him out."

The detective frowned and backed away to use his cell phone.

Mystic stood up and walked up onto the porch where Tank, Get Down and Lil Curtis had now gathered with Unc and Punkin.

When she sat down on the ledge of the porch, Tank looked at her and smiled.

"You did good girl. I'm proud of you!"

Mystic chuckled at the comment and lit up a Black & Mild. Her stomach was bubbling like crazy with nerves but she held it down. As she puffed her cigarette, she noticed the cruiser carrying Spider pulled back up in front of the house.

Spider exited the back of the car and the detective removed his cuffs. Spider looked to Mystic and nodded his head.

"I'll be right back Mommy, just let me go handle this around the corner."

He headed up Mimika and cut through the alley.

Within fifteen minutes, he was back on the block and up on the porch with the crew. When he reached her, he pulled her up off the seat and into his arms. He swallowed with his tongue and pressed himself hard against her body.

"Damn, get a room," Punkin joked.

"Fuck that, this my baby forever, you hear me? You held that shit down fo' me, real gangsta like and I'ma show you how much I appreciate it, feel me?"

Mystic smiled and nodded her head.

"Go pack an overnight bag."

Mystic rushed into the house and just started grabbing things and throwing them in the bag. She was so excited. She had stuck hood gold and she had no plans on turning back. But when she reached the top of the stairs, she paused for a moment and thought about what the officer had told her about Spider being a felon and it's consequences to her probation.

Fuck it, she thought to herself. *It's time to get what I want fo' a change.*

82

With that she headed towards the door, walked out onto the porch and never looked back. She was now ready to embark upon the journey of a lifetime or a journey that would ultimately cost her, her life.

Chapter Eleven

Cocamo lay beside Tee-Tee, both worn down and out of breath. Tee-Tee stared off at the silhouette of the street lamp, shinning into the tiny crack of the shade on Cocamo's window. She was getting more and more confused by the second. The more she spent time with him, the more her emotions were getting all mixed up. She didn't know what to think anymore.

Cocamo was always so rough and demanding to women. She didn't know how to handle the curve ball he was throwing her way. He genuinely seemed interested in her and that for some reason, made her heart smile; yet, she told herself to remain on guard with him.

Is this nigga really starting to feel me all like that or is this nigga trying to catch me off my square because of the conversation earlier concerning AJ?

Cocamo couldn't answer that question in his own head. All he knew was that he wasn't in a hurry, as usual, to throw her out his bed or his house. He reached over onto his black marbled night stand and picked his *mini* blunt out of the ashtray. He lit up his weed, took a few puffs and handed it to Tee-Tee.

Her phone began to vibrate on the floor. In her mind, she knew it was Big Slug, calling to check on both his money and his project. She definitely didn't want to answer it in front of Cocamo but if she didn't, she knew he'd be searching the hood for her within a matter of minutes. She leaned across Cocamo and her face slightly brushed up against his jimmy. It was so hard, it made Tee-Tee's mouth water. She continued to listen to the vibration coming from the side of the bed but something about the stiffness of his jimmy drew her closer and before she knew it, she had it cocked-diesel, inside her mouth.

Cocamo lay back and enjoyed the smoothness of her jaws. He closed his eyes as the mental vibe from the herbs collided with the physical vibes from her lips. He exhaled a deep breath and slid his hand across her shoulder. He glided his fingers up her neck and clinched his fist inside her hair. He used his hand to guide her head in the way he wanted to feel her lips travel against his jimmy. Tee-Tee let all kinds of thoughts flow through her mind concerning Cocamo. She understood she was sent here to get next to him to kill him, but the more she felt him, the more she began to want him.

The only problem with that was Big Slug would never let her have him. With that thought came the reality of the consequences to missing Big Slug's phone call. Tee-Tee knew she had to return it, quickly. She put emphasis on the way her jaw muscles began to massage his jimmy. Used her tongue to tickle the top of it. Relaxed her muscles and forced it to the back of her throat.

Cocamo responded just as she'd hoped. He gripped her by the back of the head, began to gyrate his waist and thrust his jimmy deeper into her mouth. Within minutes, she had what she wanted, a quick release and Cocamo had what he wanted. He had delivered her a protein shake.

Tee-Tee looked up to Cocamo and told him she needed to get back out on the block.

"I don't want no shit from his big ass."

Cocamo shook his head and said he understood.

"Time is money baby. Do you. Shit, I'm good. You took care of me already, now go take care of that nigga thats street pimpin' you. I'll get at you again."

Tee-Tee heard the spite in Cocamo's voice and her feelings were a little hurt but she also knew that that was the way Cocamo was. He would never let you know what he was feeling. Sarcasm was always his best defense.

Yet and still, Tee-Tee couldn't believe Cocamo could still be that way to her, so rough like he just didn't give a damn that they'd just got through fucking. She didn't have time to get into it with him at the moment. She had to get to the block.

She grabbed her clothes, excused herself to the bathroom and began to get dressed. When she re-entered the room, Cocamo pretended like he'd fallen asleep. Tee-Tee knew he was just avoiding having to talk to her on her way out. She let him have it... she politely grabbed her purse, headed for the front door, walked out and closed it behind her.

Once outside, she immediately walked down the steps, reached inside her purse and grabbed her phone. She looked at the *recent calls* and sure enough, Big Slug had called, twice. She knew he'd be out on the hunt for her as she began to sprint across Mimika towards Harney. The headlights almost blinded her as they approached her from out of no where it seemed. By the time she could hop onto the curb, she already knew who it was.

The Suburban came to a screeching halt beside her, the passenger side window came roaring down, the stereo turned down to a whisper.

"Get yo' ass in here, bitch!"

Cocamo lay in his bed, wondering why he was tripping off of Tee-Tee so much. *She ain't all that*, he kept trying to reason with himself. But for some reason, no matter how hard he tried to convince himself of that, he was starting to dig her. But he couldn't deal with a woman that got up and ran at the beck-n-call of another nigga. That, his *hood* status wouldn't allow.. And as long as she was under Big Slug's thumb, he had to treat just as what she was, just another hoe.

Chapter Twelve

The truck pulled up to the Western Inn Hotel and the intersection of Jennings Station Rd and Hwy 70. Spider looked at Mystic and turned up the volume to the stereo he reached across the console and ran his hand slowly up her thigh. He moved her burgundy flowered sundress to the side and began to sing the words to **R Kelly's** *Never Leave*, as he plunged his fingers inside her.

"... I will never leave you, you don't worry, girl I'll be right there fo' you. I will never leave, no, God put us together, nothin' can take that away. I will ne-e-e-ever leave..."

If the way he was finger fucking her didn't have her in such a trans, she would have found such humor in the way he sounded. Spider thrust harder and harder, loving the wetness he felt pouring from Mystic's mommy. He spoke to as she moaned at his touch.

"You know you my baby, right?"

Mystic panted.

"You know I'ma take care of you, right? Give you what you need, what you want?"

He curved his fingers and Mystic moans increased.

"You ain't never gotta worry about no muthafucka doin' nothin' to hurt you, you hear me? I got this, this shit right here..."

He bent his elbow and Mystic felt his fingers touch her cervix. Her moans became extremely vocal.

"... this mines. And I'ma take damn good care of it, bet yo' life on that shit."

He stuck his tongue in her ear as he added another finger. Mystic leaned her head back and let it go. Her juices flowed all over his fingers and Spiders jimmy pulsated in his shorts.

Mystic looked at him as he tasted her essence. He amazed her, he set off places in her body she didn't know existed and she loved it... she needed it. And for it, she would do anything to keep it.

The hotel room was equipped with a queen sized bed and a Jacuzzi. He instructed her to get comfortable and he'd be right back. He had to make a run. He returned with dozen of roses he'd ran up to the Schnucks on West Florissant to buy. He gave her six of the roses and told her the other six was for their Jacuzzi bath.

He leaned down to kiss her and Mystic could still taste her juices on his tongue. The erotic flavor drove her crazy. Spider went into the bathroom, ran the water in the Jacuzzi, ripped the petals off the stems and threw them into the water.

He had picked up some scented candles and strategically placed them on the ends of the tub and the top of the toilet bowl. He killed the lights and closed the door behind him. He walked back into the bedroom and grabbed Mystic by the hand. He led her to the bathroom, opened the door from behind her and smiled as she gasped at the sight.

He began to undress her, sliding the straps off her shoulders and down her arms. He watched the sundress fall to the floor, exposing her plump, round ass in the glow of the candle light. He reached around her and began to massage her breasts firmly with his hands.

Mystic's mouth watered at the feel of his touch and the hardness he had pressed against the crease of her ass. Its stiffness made her want to taste it, feel it. Spider slid his hands down her waist and with one finger on each hand, slid her panties down to the floor.

He inhaled her scent on his way down and wanted it. He kneeled down and began to place soft kisses on her ass cheeks. The gentle nibbles almost made her knees buckle. He turned her to face him, looked at the pretty cookie in front of him then looked up to her. Mystic returned his gaze through anxious and wanting eyes.

"Wait!" she said, holding up her hands. "I got something for you."

She ran around him, out the bathroom. She went over to her purse, grabbed the folded piece of notebook paper and opened it. She walked over to him.

"Now, I'm kinda shy about my poetry and so you'd betta not laugh. I'm sensitive about my shit."

He leaned against the door frame and smiled.

"I promise, I won't laugh. Do yo' thang, Mommy."

Mystic stood back and began to read what she had written for him.

A Thug-A-Boo is two sided, multi-complexed black man,
Who can hold the heart and soul of any black woman, securely within the palm of his hands.

On one side, he's rough and hardcore, reppin' the streets down to the bone.
On the other side, he's as gentle as a newborn baby, when he and his woman are alone.

When the block is quiet, his grind is done and he's laid the streets to rest,
He is that same Thug-A-Boo, stroking his woman's hair, as she lies gracefully upon his chest.

In the streets he's gutta, for static he don't play, he'll even take your life if he must.

He's the best of both worlds, puttin' in work on both the streets and in the bed, from dawn to dusk.

A sometimes, pistol packin', always jeans half-saggin, hood version of Al Capone'.

But in the heat of the passion, he's gives lovin' so raw, he brings multiple orgasms so strong.

Whoever said that a Thug-A-Boo, is the world's greatest failure, simply could not have been telling the truth.

For they have never tasted the pleasure of lovin', a Thug-A-Boo like you.

****

She bit the bottom of her lip and stared down at the floor. She was afraid to look at him.

"So, what did you think?"

He walked over to her, lifted her face to his and kissed her. In between the passion, he told her that he thought it was beautiful. He told her he thought she was beautiful. He told her it was the sweetest thing anyone had ever done for him.

He turned her back to the bathroom.

"Back up, let the top down on the toilet and sit down."

She blew out the cabdle on the back of the tank and did as he instructed her and watched as Spider crawled to her like a lion approaching his prey. He was so sexy to her. When he reached her he took her left leg and mounted it up on the ledge of the tub and told her to lean back. When she did, it exposed the humongous clit at the top of her fat and pretty mommy. Its juices, glistening in the candle light.

Spider closed in on his target, wrapped his lips around her clit, tightened his jaws and began to suck on it like a newborn baby attacking its mother's nipple. Spider ripped her clit apart, pouncing on it with his tongue.

Mystic squirmed at the intensity she felt between her legs. Her thighs tightened, her foot slipped off the tub and her body released orgasm number two on the night. She wanted to please him in return, let him know that she wanted him and only him. He stood up in front of her but as she leaned in to greet his jimmy with her tongue, he backed away.

Spider snatched her from the seat and spent her around.

"It ain't about me, it's about you. You stepped up to the plate today even after you found out about my situation. You had my back, now I'm about to have yours."

He threw her down by her back, forward onto the toilet. He kicked her leg to the side and slammed into her. It was heaven to him. It was so hot and wet inside her, Spider knew he wouldn't be able to maintain for long. He decided to make his presence known. He thrust inside her harder and harder, pounding to her screams of pleasure. She made it clear to him what she wanted.

"Go deeper, go deeper, baby."

He placed her leg up onto the toilet seat, turning her body side ways. He had an all access path to her guts and to pleasure. She could feel him in her stomach and she loved it. Every stroke shaved off a day she was locked down and pent up with sexual frustration.

He grabbed her by the back of her head as he reached his peak and felt hers build. When he knew she was about to blow, he pulled her up to him and grabbed her by the throat from behind. He tightened his grip as they both unloaded their juices, intertwining with the other.

He panted, she panted... his heart pulsated, hers tripled... they were exhausted. Spider guided Mystic into the tub behind him and as they both kneeled down into the hot water, Spider pulled her close to him. She leaned back onto his chest and sighed. She locked her fingers into his.

"So, were you gon' tell me?"

"I was gon' tell you, mommy, once I found out if you was real or not. Hoes is crazy out here and a nigga can't afford to be attached to a bitch with "S-P.""

"What's S-P?"

"Stalka Potential."

Mystic chuckled.

"Check this Lil Mama, a man gon' do what he do, regardless. But as long as he pay the bills and handle home, it don't matter. I'm out here riskin' my life er' day on these streets. You see that shit today. If it wasn't fo' you... anyway, I'm takin' all the risks to keep food on the table and a roof over our head. So naw, can't nobody chain me down. But that don't mean that I don't have respect fo' home, that's why I'm picky about who I fuck wit' and let in my circle.

But you, you showed me, just how gutta you are today and a nigga that's out here on the grind and puttin' in work, need a woman like that on his side. That's why I wanna take you outta town with me this weekend to handle some business, you down?"

Did he just say, outta town?

Mystic knew that by her being on probation, she was required to put in for permission to travel two weeks in advance and provide all the details of her itinerary. If she was caught, automatic revocation.

"Whatever happened to, not havin' me around what you do?" she asked him, sitting up.

"Would you rather I take someone else?"

She weighed the consequences against all she could gain from going with him. She would undeniably earn all the brownie points she would need, to be his number one and to Mystic, that's all that mattered. She turned to him.

"I'll go anywhere you need me to go with you."

She leaned in to place a seductive kiss on his lips. Slowly, she moved down his neck and his chest. She glanced up at him and smiled.

"Let's see how long I can hold my breath."

With that, she disappeared under the water.

Chapter Thirteen

Big Slug snatched Tee-Tee up into the truck when she opened to door and began to climb inside.

"You better pray like hell, you either did one or two muthafuckin' thangs tonight. You either better have a substantial amount of my money or that nigga betta be layin' up in there twisted sideways. And since I don't see no muthafuckin' ambulance, I'm gon' assume you got some stacks fo' me and not just a funky, wet ass. Do I fuckin' look like a nigga that's got all this muthafuckin' time on my hands to be sittin' here blowin' yo phone up like that? Bitch I'm busy, I got shit to do!"

"You said get next to him... this shit ain't easy. This nigga ain't just one of these lame ass nigga's round here. He on guard. What the fuck you want me do, just go to war with the nigga? You think I'm soft on this nigga? You think I like being used up and thrown away like a muthafuckin' dirty tampon? I workin' on it, shit!"

"Let me tell you somethin', I don't give a fuck what you gotta do, how you gotta do it or how many fuckin' times it takes for you to do it. I gave you a job to do, now if you ain't that bitch handle it. I can move muthafuckin' mountains Tee and do somethin' different. I thought you was about this paper. I thought you wanted to do something different fo' that lil bitch of a baby round that corner. I thought you was in this to win this."

"First of all, I *am* in this to win it and second of all, don't you ever call my baby out her fuckin' name again!"

The blow came so quick, she really didn't have to react. Big Slug had just made her see stars inside the Suburban with a deadly stroke of his hand.

"Who the fuck do you think you talkin' to. You don't run shit out here in these streets bitch! I call you and any other muthafucka what I want too. These my streets, feel me. And to teach you that, get the fuck out my truck and get yo' funky pussy ass down the way and make my money. All of it, no shorts, feel me?"

Tee-Tee rubbed the side of her face as she stared down to her purse, lying on her lap. The thought of killing his fat ass had crossed her mind so many times, but it was running rampart at the moment. She couldn't believe he had put his hands on her. Nothing would make her happier than to see his blood splattered all over his precious leather seats. Instead, she resigned and opened the passenger side door and slid down off the seat. She had to eat, no lie. She wasn't financially able to challenge him at that moment but she held on to the hope that one day her money would be right and he would be dead.

Tee-Tee waited until Big Slug turned onto Shulte before she began to walk down Mimika towards her people. She looked over at Cocamo's house as she passed by. Something inside her told her to go and knock on his window. Wake him up and tell him what Big Slug had put her up too. But she knew that wasn't an option. Cocamo didn't care anything about her so why would she risk her life to save his. This was all about business, nothing personal. So no matter how good he put it down or made her feel, killing him meant her survival.

Tee-Tee walked down to the corner of Mimika and Lenora Avenue, where she ran into Lil' Curtis and Harvey, chillin' on the porch of Lil' Curtis' house.

"Whaddup T-Baby? Where the fuck you been? That big polish eatin' muthafucka been round here lookin' fo' you. I told that big sumo ass nigga, I ain't know where you was at, go eat a muthafuckin' bear or somethin', big ass muthafucka. You can hear his fat ass breathin' over the radio."

95

Tee-Tee laughed at Lil' Curtis. He was definitely one of the craziest nigga's on the block. But he was also a hustla and she needed him to help her get off the stones in her pocket. She needed an *"el"* first so she suggested they walk to the Phillips 66 on West Florissant and Park Lane. Lil' Curtis however wanted a drink so they walked down to JMar's Liquor Store at the corner of Riverview and West Florissant. They shot the shit with Toi and Hank for a minute then headed back up the way to make some money.

They posted up on the porch as Tee-Tee began to tell him about the situation with Cocamo and Big Slug. Tee-Tee knew Lil' Curtis talked a lot of shit around the hood but he would never put her out there nor tell her secrets. They were way too cool for that. Lil' Curtis shook his head.

"Let's duct tape a water hose in that big nigga's mouth and watch his muthafuckin' stomach blow up and shoot out bacon –n- pork chops er'where."

They chuckled as Tee-Tee handed him the blunt and checked out the approaching vehicle. The tan Mazda pulled down the street at about six mph and Tee-Tee knew it was a clucker looking for a stone. Lil' Curtis checked out the car and told Tee-Tee not to fuck with it.

"Two white muthafucka's in the hood this time of night? You know them muthafucka's UC's (Under Cover's)."

Tee-Tee waved him off.

"I done seen them round here before. Buck 'nem fuck with them all the time."

Lil' Curtis felt uneasy as he watched Tee-Tee approach the car and make the sale. He felt even more uneasy as he saw the headlight cut on from two cars parked on the corner of Floy and Lenora. He looked back to Harvey.

"Shit nigga, move out the muthafuckin' way, here come them boys!"

Harvey and Lil' Curtis both darted into the house and peeped out the curtain. They watched as the two cars, locked and loaded with "the jump-out-boyz," jumped down on Tee-Tee as the Mazda pulled away.

"Man, didn't I just tell her dumb ass not to sell shit to them cracka's. Talkin' bout, Buck 'nem fuck with 'em. Who the fuck round here don't know Buck 'nem *is* the muthafuckin' police. Them nigga's been slangin' dope out here for decades and never seen the inside of a cell. So what that tell you?"

Tee-Tee hung her head as the female officer stuck her hand down inside Tee-Tee pocket's and pulled out the remaining stones. She did however, breathe a sign of relief that her purse with her gun, was on Lil' Curtis' porch and without permission, they couldn't go get it. She was no longer on their property.

As the female officer cuffed her, a black officer with an apparent case of male pattern baldness, asked Tee-Tee if she wanted to make this easier on herself.

"A small fish in a big pond and I don't really give a fuck about small fish. I'm into the big catch. So what about it? You that loyal to Big Slug?"

Tee-Tee just looked off at the ground. There was no way she was about to turn on Big Slug for a few stones. Then what? What happens when he post bail? He would and Tee-Tee knew her life would be over.

"I don't know no Big Slug," she told the man.

"Have it your way."

97

Lil' Curtis and Harvey came back onto the porch as they were placing Tee-Tee in the back of the squad car. He looked down at her purse on the top step. She shook her head "no" to let him know not to fuck with her shit but she also knew he would eventually go through it with a fine tooth comb. As soon as the police car hit the corner, he did just as she thought. He opened the purse and smiled at his new, shiny item for sale, Tee-Tee's pistol. She didn't have any money inside her purse but she did give him a name to work with as far as getting her out... Cocamo.

"Aey, nigga, I'll be right back. Come out my house and lock up my shit. You know you steal, nigga. Hands so sticky, you'd think ya momma's anionic fluid was super glue." He told Harvey.

Lil' Curtis and Harvey locked up the house with Tee-Tee's purse in tow and took off walking up Mimika towards Harney. They crossed the street and came to a stop at the house with the multicolored bricks. Lil' Curtis walked up on the porch and knocked on the door.

Chapter Fourteen

The trip to Indy took all of three and a half hours. Spider rented a mid-sized Toyota Camry for the weekend trip. He didn't want to ride in anything that would draw attention to them. Before pulling out, he stopped on Martin Luther King Blvd., at the Lee's Pawn and Jewelry to purchase Mystic a wedding band similar to the one he wore on his left hand.

Funny how I didn't even notice that before, Mystic thought to herself. Spider wanted the appearance of a newlywed couple, out on a weekend of fun together. He had taken several women on this trip with him before but he never cared enough about them to let them know what exactly the trips were about or what type of risks they were taking by going with him. By the time they realized they transporting pounds of weed, it was too late. They were already committed to the game. Most didn't complain though, the free trip and the few hundred dollars he gave them upon returning to St. Louis, pretty much kept them good.

But this trip, he was going to enjoy. He was taking someone he was coming to care about very much, maybe even too much. Which was the reason, he decided to let her know the ends and outs of the business they were going to handle.

Mystic looked down at the band on her finger. She didn't care if it was just all apart of the plan to Spider, it meant something to her. No one had ever given her a ring before, role playing or not. Mystic twisted the band around her finger and smiled to herself.

Spider dialed the number to his connect on the phone to let him know they had arrived at the Holiday Inn on South Keystone Avenue in downtown Indy. Spider turned to Mystic when he hung up the phone and began explaining what to expect from the meeting.

"Look Mommy, these nigga's is kinda shady. Stay close to me, don't say nothin'; just chill, ok? These some nigga's my cousin fuck with on the green tip and er' time I come up to this muthafucka I get uneasy dealin' with these nigga's. But..."

He patted the side of his waist.

"...You safe wit' me, Boo. It's good."

As Spider knocked on the door to room *217*, Mystic's cell phone began to ring. It was Punkin. Spider shook his head.

"No phones, Boo. These nigga's see you on the phone and they think you on the line settin' them up and shit."

Mystic looked at Spider confused.

"It's just Punkin baby. I'm sure she's just callin' to make sure we made it."

"They don't know that, they don't know Punkin. Trust me mommy."

Mystic returned the phone to the back pocket of her jeans and stood off to the back of Spider. When the door opened, a twenty-something-year-old, light skinned man, greeted them.

"Whud-dup fam?"

His eyes were bloodshot red, no doubt from the strong odor of Budda that hit you as soon as the door opened. He extended his hand to Spider and gave him some dap. He looked off to Mystic and nodded his head. They were used to Spider bringing young girls up on the trip with him, most for a little extra cash, they were able to fuck.

"Who dat?"

"Mines," Spider responded, winking his eye at Mystic. That statement made her feel good. It was always something about a woman wanting to be the woman of the most popular guy in school, in the hood, or in his crew. It made them feel important to be the one on his arm, this was no different. Mystic loved to hear him claim her. With that statement, he knew she was not for sale.

The scraggly looking man Spider referred to as "Remo," moved to the side and allowed them entrance to the room. Inside there were two other, dark skinned men, puffing on blunts and drinking Crown. Everyone greeted each other and got right down to business.

"The Lou must be poppin', this the third time we seen you in a month," the chubby one said, displaying a mouth full of Platinum teeth.

"It's good, you know how we do it in the hood. It's ain't about how many muthafucka's you know that smoke, it's about how many could you possibly know that don't."

"True dat," Remo echoed, toasting his blunt in the air and starring at Mystic.

He was undressing her with his eyes. Mystic could feel him virtually staring through her and it made it uncomfortable. Not wanting to alarm Spider, recalling what he told her in the car and the hallway, Mystic just slowly moved closer to him.

Spider responded as she had hoped he would and placed his arm around her neck. That made Remo chuckle to himself.

"Anyway fam, I got yo' shit packed just the way you like it. It's that *Death* too nigga, I know you don't smoke no mo', so take it from us, *this shit right here*, this that killa. Watch them roads out there too my nigga, them boys been crackin' down on er' thang movin'."

"Careful is my middle name, homie."

"You stayin' and clubbin'?" Remo asked.

"Naw, not this time playa, I got other plans," Spider said, reaching down into his pockets and pulling out two stacks of money laced together with a rubber band. He tossed the money on the bed and gave each one of his business partners some love. He looked to Mystic and told her to open the door as he grabbed to suitcase out the corner.

On her way to the door, she passed Remo, who stuck out his tongue and traced it around his lips.

"Nice meeting you, Ma. Hope to see you again."

Spider hit him playfully on his chest and chuckled.

"Calm down nigga. It's like Hammer baby, you can't touch that."

Remo sucked his teeth and stood up to close the door behind them. Remo despised Spider secretly on the inside. If it wasn't for his friend, Spider's cousin Cam, he would been set him up to get jacked on one of these trips. Remo was the jealous type. He didn't want no one doing better than him, in any shape form or fashion, especially with the ladies. With Spider, it was the fact that he got thrown in the background every time Spider came in town. Spider was the life of the party and an out-of-towner and so the Indy women flocked to him.

Remo, crated faced with a face full of pits, crooked teeth and bad breath that often put the females he came in contact with, in the mind frame of *"Bilal"* from *"House Party."* He often had to put out for meat. He hated that. Spider often sensed his distaste for him but Spider played his game by the code of the streets: Keep yo' friends close and yo' enemies, closer.

As they exited the hotel lobby Mystic's phone rung again. It was Punkin again. Mystic listened attentively through the ear piece to Punkin's conversation, as Spider went into the gas station to pay for the fuel.

"...they shot him six times I think. But it was real fucked up how it went down. Word in the hood is, it got back that he had somethin' to do with that Curly shit. Caught him standin' out in front of Harney and let loose. I thought you might wanna tell him befo' he get back and hear it from over these ways."

Mystic's eyes welled up with tears. How was she going to tell Spider someone had killed his long time friend. When he was done pumping the gas, he took a seat inside the car beside her.

"So, what's good, mommy? What you wanna do? We can go eat, hit the club, get a room and chill fo' the night, it's whatever as long as I got you."

Mystic let the tears fall and Spider grabbed her thigh.

"What's wrong? Why you cryin'? What Punkin say?"

Mystic looked out the window in front of her. She couldn't bring herself to look at him and say something she knew would hurt him.

"Talk to me, Boo. What's good? I don't like that look on yo' face. Did I do somethin', did that scene scare you or make you uncomfortable back there? Or is it that you trippin' cause you outta state?"

Mystic shook her head.

"Pun... Punkin called and said that somebody got hurt. Somebody close to you."

Spider's mind instinctively went to Tank or Perez. He gripped the steering wheel, bracing himself for the blow.

"Who," he asked, softly.

"Get Down."

"What?" he asked, looking confused.

"Who the fuck would be stupid enough to fuck wit' my nigga, Get Down?"

"From what Punkin said, somebody went back and told them nigga's on Sherry that he had somethin' to do wit' what went down after Kay Kay got killed. Shot him six times on the corner of Mimika and Harney."

Spider exhaled a deep breath and looked to Mystic. He was already plottin' his payback when he reached the 314 area code. Get Down was his closest friend, besides Perez and Tank. They had done a lot of dirt together.

How fucked up is that, they got him for the one he didn't do, Spider thought to himself. He hit Mystic on the thigh and asked her if it would be okay if they got a room for the night and headed out the next day.

"I ain't in grind mode right now, Boo and I gotta be focused to get you and this shit to the crib safely, you hear me?"

"Its good baby, I understand."

Chapter Fifteen

Lil Curtis knocked on the widow to the brown front door and waited patiently for Cocamo to open it. He looked down at Tee-Tee's purse and remembered the gun inside. He quickly removed the tiny .22 and placed it in the back of his waist line. He finally heard the lock turn on the door and he stepped back so Cocamo could get a clear view of him. He knew Cocamo was crazy, let alone trigger happy and the last thing he wanted to do, was get shot.

"Whaddup Cocamo," Lil' Curtis said, as Cocamo stretched in the doorway before coming outside onto the porch.

"What's good nigga?"

"I came to holla at you bout' ol' girl."

"Who?" Cocamo asked.

"Tee-Tee, them jump out boys just got her. Making a sell to some cracka ass UC's in front of the crib. I was gon go tell her momma and shit but, I already know she ain't gon' go and get her. So, I figured since you smashin' her…"

"Who the fuck told you that?" Cocamo asked, sort of offensive.

"Nigga, er' body round here know you tappin' that. Nigga this Mimika, this the block that don't sleep. You ain't gotta front fo' me. Hell, I been tryin' to hit since we was in diapers nigga, so I'm jealous! So anyway, she left her purse on my step and so I just thought it might contain somethin' she might need *and* a small reward for myself."

"Reward? Nigga, Tee-Tee ain't my gal, she ain't even my bottom bitch, what the fuck do I care bout her being locked up. Pussy is pussy. Shit, just like I tap that, I'll tap another. Bitches is like illegal cable nigga, when Charter do a sweep and cut yo' supply off, you get on the horn and find another nigga to restore yo' service."

Lil' Curtis waved his hand at Cocamo. He knew he was just talking shit because it was him he was talking too. He sat Tee-Tee's purse down on the ledge of the porch and began walking down the front steps.

"Cocamo man, gone with all that ghetto philosopizin' and shit. She gon' end up downtown and them people's open all night."

Cocamo walked over to ledge, picked up her purse and looked inside.

"Aey, where's her heat? Did she have it on her when they got her?"

Lil' Curtis did his best *Smokey* impression from Friday.

"Aww yeah, you know I be high Cocamo, you know I be fucked up."

He reached in his back waist line and handed Cocamo the .22 and hit him on the leg.

"I know that's gotta be worth somethin' to you man. Gone, hook ya boy up with a lil somethin', somethin'. You know JMar's still open."

Cocamo reached down in his shorts pocket and pulled out a ten dollar bill.

"It's all I got."

Lil' Curtis took the ten and headed down the steps.

"I know it ain't all you got, you cheap muthafucka but it's enough."

Cocamo chuckled, walked back inside the house and sat down on the couch. He thought long and hard about what he should do. He was right when he told Lil' Curtis that she wasn't his woman. Why would he go bail her out just because she gave him some pussy?

Shit, that shit's a dime a dozen, he thought to himself. He looked inside her purse and pulled out the picture of the little girl. He stared at her. She resembled her mother in so many ways. About an hour had passed since he'd gotten the news of Tee-Tee being locked up. Cocamo exhaled a deep breath, placed the picture back inside the purse, stood up and walked into his bedroom.

He opened his closet, reached up and grabbed the grey, Nike shoebox and placed it on top of his bed. He pulled out his cell phone, reached in Tee-Tee's purse, grabbed her ID and left to retrieve the phone book from the dining room. He searched through the white pages until he found the number to the Justice Center downtown.

"Yeah, uhh, I would like to know if you got a, Telisa Banks in custody and if so, when will she have a bail hearing."

The clerk placed him on hold while she searched the database for Tee-Tee's name.

"Yes, she's being booked in right now. She'll see the Judge in the morning via satellite. She should have a bail amount by eight o'clock."

"Aight, thanks."

Cocamo hung up the phone and reached over onto the night stand to grab his weed tray and a blunt. He rolled up a stogie and lay back to decide if he really wanted to do this. This could have complications he wasn't ready for. She would think things he wasn't sure he was ready for her to think. Foxy 95.5 was still pumping out the hits and Cocamo just wanted to get some type of clarity on what he was feeling.

"Oh Lord, what did I do to deserve her? Heaven knows, Lord knows I'm only human. Can this be someone truly for me? Or is it a cruel fantasy? Cause nothing has ever felt, like this..."

Will Downing laid down the music and forced Cocamo to search his soul. What was he really feeling for her? He both liked and respected her grind. He liked the way she made him feel in bed. But he didn't think she was strong enough to be seriously in his life. For Cocamo to have a woman in his life, past his bedroom, she would have to be virtually made of steel. He needed a backbone. Tee-Tee seemed to be inferior when it came to Big Slug and the streets.

She moved when he told her to move and that in a woman, Cocamo couldn't tolerate. He was used to having control in every single aspect of his life, including his woman. Tee-Tee was just not what he was looking for, or so he thought.

Chapter Sixteen

Once inside the room, Mystic lay back propped up on pillows with Spider lying across her lap. She stroked his head as he talked about his friend.

"He wasn't gangsta like that but if he was ever pushed into a corner, the nigga always came out swingin'. Good nigga too, Boo, you hear me? I ain't never known that nigga to throw salt on me. Loyal... he was loyal to the bone. You know I'ma kill them nigga's, right? Wipe out they whole muthafuckin' generation when I hit the block. It's a done deal."

"I figured."

Mystic stroked his face. He rose up and walked outside to stand on the balcony. She sat there a minute, then walked outside to be with him.

"I'm sorry baby, I'm so sorry you're hurting."

"I'm pissed off," he said turning to her.

His voice began to waiver and Mystics' heart began to break. She walked up behind him and wrapped her arms around his waist. She laid her head on his back. She knew that it took a lot for him to let his emotions flow, especially in front of her and she took that to heart. She let him vent, as she rubbed her hands up and down his chest.

"When I find 'em, I'ma kill 'em, no questions asked. These muthafucka's are so dead when I come across 'em," he said, continuing to hit his hand against the rail.

Mystic began to massage his chest and continuously kissed him on his back. He turned to face her and looked at her. She could see so many emotions flowing through him. Rage, for the nigga's who'd hurt his friend. Pain, from losing someone so close to him.

Vulnerability, from releasing his emotions out in the open for her to see. Need, the need to be held, caressed and understood.

"You know I'ma kill 'em, don't you?"

Mystic nodded her head as she leaned in, to place a soft kiss on his cheek and gripped him around his neck.

"Stick a fork in them nigga's cause they done Boo, you hear me? They done! You know that, right?"

Mystic opened her mouth and kissed him again, this time with a moist tongue against his skin.

Spider snatched his face back and told her to turn around. His goal, to release as much emotion into Mystic as he could, didn't matter how he did it. He bent her down over the rail and Mystic almost lost control of her knees when he thrust his oversized jimmy inside her. He was angry, he was enraged, he was hurt and he was determined to make her feel it.

She gripped the rail as tight as she could and bit down on the bottom of her lip and he plunged deep inside her. She didn't care if he had no romance. She loved every stroke he dished out and she could do nothing but stare out into the courtyard, with her own fantasy playing in her mind. Smiling at the people passing by as she came long and hard against his jimmy. The fresh air gave her a sense of heaven as she inhaled it, deeply.

Spider continued to pound inside her and she could feel him swell tremendously as he came closer to his peak. Mystic began to gyrate her hips in a circular motion and dip down as to engulf him, all his hurt, all his anger and all his pain, deeply into her mommy as he dug into her shoulders and moaned.

He reached up and squeezed her breast with force.

"I'm mad as a muthafucka."

He slammed inside her, hard and fierce.

"I'm a hurt me a muthafucka."

His tears were now coming down his face.

"I need you. I need you to stop me from killin' a muthafucka."

His nails dig into her skin.

"Come on baby, come on. You can take it out on me. Give me all yo' hurt and all yo' anger. You wanna kill somethin', you can... kill yo' pussy."

BOOM! He unloaded inside her, laid his head on her back and cried.

Chapter Seventeen

As the music continued to play, Cocamo thought of all the different ways he could spin the fact of him, getting Tee-Tee out of jail. He wasn't too concerned with the money, The fact that if flowed through his hands like a continuous stream of water meant nothing. Deep inside he knew Tee-Tee would pay him back, with interest.

It was the underlying message that seemed to confuse him the most. Coming to her rescue would undoubtedly be like admitting to himself that she was somehow different than any other woman he bedded.

This bitch is getting' to me, he told himself as he clicked off his light and laid back on his pillow. He could still smell her scent of Baby Phat on his sheets. He closed his eyes, tried to go to sleep but all he could do is think of her. The way her hair smelled, the way she rode him, the way she kissed his body. Cocamo had never told anyone before but no woman has ever made him cum with oral sex... no one but Tee-Tee.

He wouldn't giver her the satisfaction though, of letting her know this. It played over and over again in his head. She honestly had all the qualities that he could want in a woman. He was just too set in his ways to accept it.

He climbed out of bed and went into the living room where Unc was now sitting on the couch. He had just returned from next door at Punkin's house. Cocamo sat down on the couch across from him and asked Unc to pour him a shot of what he was drinking. Unc poured Cocamo a shot of Patron in a glass and handed it to him.

"You look like you got somethin' on yo' mind nephew; you good?" Unc asked him, firing up a blunt Cocamo left in the ashtray earlier.

Cocamo took a hard swallow of the liquor and sat up on the edge of the seat cushion.

"Let me ask you somethin' Unc; how do you know when you really feelin' somebody?"

"You mean, feelin' as in, *wantin'* to fuck wit 'em?"

"Yeah I mean, after auntie died, you said you couldn't see yo'self fuckin' wit' nobody else but now... Punkin got you slippin' in and outta her crib, I guess my question is, how'd you get yo' self to go against what yo' mind said, *don't do* and do it anyway?"

Unc sat back on the seat and stared off into the ceiling. He chuckled at the thought of him and Punkin.

"Neph, Punkin and I ain't never fucked. Believe it or not. I mean, don't get me wrong, I rub up against all that ass and them big ol' titties all the time but we ain't never got further than that. It's not cause of yo' auntie neither. Punkin is one of the coolest bitches I know and I don't wanna lose that friendship with her.

Sometimes, you gotta put yo' own needs to the side and do what's best overall. Sometimes that immediate shit can fuck up some long-term shit that could've been beautiful, had the immediate shit not happened, understand?"

Cocamo laughed.

"Uhh, I think so. Shit, did you unda'stand that shit?"

"Perfectly, Neph. But then I ain't the one sittin' here stressin' out over a woman either." Unc told him, placing his hand on Cocamo's shoulder. "Follow yo' instincts Neph. You a hustla, if you don't know about anything else, you know how to trust yo' gut."

113

What Unc had told him seemed to make a world of sense to Cocamo. He knew that bailing Tee-Tee out of jail would be beneficial to him in more than one way. It would be good business wise because he would make sure he taxed her for the inconvenience. Personally, it would give him an opportunity to figure out what it was that continued to draw him to her. To figure out what it was about her that demanded his time and his thoughts.

It was settled, he would make her bond hearing in a few hours at The Justice Center. Once he finalized that decision within himself, it was as if a heavy burden had lifted from off is mind and he dozed off within minutes but not before he thought of her, once again.

Chapter Eighteen

As the rented Camry made a left turn off West Florissant onto Mimika, Spider looked to the top of the hill and noticed the familiar white, four door undercover car. Sitting behind the stop sign at the corner of Mimika and Shulte, the two white male detectives lay in wait for what they assumed would be the black Suburban to hit the corner.

When Spider saw them in the distance, he quickly pulled over to the curb. He looked over to Mystic and patted her on the side of her thigh, aggressively.

"Get out, mommy."

Mystic followed his eyes up the street and tried to see what he saw but the Ford Explorer parked in front of them, was blocking her view, He seemed kind of nervous to her and she wanted to know why.

Maybe he sees his wife up there, she reasoned with herself. She understood that in the game, she had to play her role and her role as of that moment was the role of the "bitch on the side," meaning she knew she had to bow down whenever it came to *wifey.*

"Why?"

"Cause… just do it. I need you to get out the car and walk up the street. Wait 'til you see my car cut the corner before you start walkin', aight?"

Mystic began to utter as Spider put up his hand to stop her.

"Mommy, don't do this right now. If I tell you something, trust and believe it's fo' yo' own good. Just like last night."

Mystic resigned and reached for the handle of the passenger side door and began to step out of the car.

"Aey... aey, babygirl, just trust it and no mater what happens, this right here, 'tween me and you... is real, you heard me?"

Mystic felt herself begin to panic. She didn't like the way he was sounding.

What the fuck is he seein'? And what does he mean whatever happens?

Mystic looked at Spider one last time before she closed the door to the Camry and stepped back onto the side walk. She watched sadly as he pulled off and headed up the block.

Mystic took a deep breath and as he instructed her, she began walking the moment she saw him hit the corner, followed by the white car. When she reached the front steps, she realized that her bags were still in the trunk of the rental car and that wasn't a good thing.

"Why you walkin'?" Punkin asked, as Mystic sat down on the ledge of the porch.

Punkin was hittin' her blunt and cutting her toe nails. Mystic hunched her shoulders.

"I don't know. He saw somethin' up the way that he didn't like and he told me to get out the car down the block and wait 'til I see him hit the corner and start walkin'. I thought maybe he saw his wife or somethin'."

Punkin chuckled.

"Naw, he don't care nothin' bout that. Real nigga's, the ones that game the game on lock, keep they bitches at the crib under control."

"So I hear," Mystic replied.

Punkin puffed her blunt and choked. She started coughing like she was stricken with the whooping cough virus.

116

"Girl, nigga's don't really care about them broads at home. It just goes to the game they in. Most of 'em just need a woman so they got somewhere to call home. They don't really care too much about the woman herself but the fact that they got shelter when they get through fuckin' around in these streets. Most of they hoes at home look a hot mess. But that means that he can do what he do and she ain't gon' say shit cause she got a man, that can have any other woman but he chose her. And she knows at the drop of a dime, he can leave her.

Take Breeze and Man for example. Man don't care nothin' 'bout her dumb ass fo' real. He just uses her to transport his shit. How many bitches he runnin' around here fuckin'? And she know it, you'd have to be one dumb ass bitch, not to know that nigga layin' down dick all across the hood. But because she wants the material benefits, she sucks that shit up. She turns the other cheek."

Mystic inhaled Punkin's words as she fiddled with her fingers in her lap. Her eyes trailed off as Toi and Hank came running around the corner and straight towards them. They stopped short of Mystic in front of Unc's house.

Toi, panting and out of breath, held her hand up to get Mystic's attention.

"They got Spider in front of his house."

"What?" Mystic said, jumping up off the ledge.

The tone in Toi's voice carried loudly and brought Unc from his living room to the porch.

"Who got Spider?" he said. Looking over to Punkin and Mystic.

"Them UC's that was parked over here on Shulte. They rushed him as soon as he stepped out the car round the corner. It's like fiddy po-po's up in they crib right now. They got the wife, kids, all of 'em on the curb, cuffed."

So that's what he saw, the UC's, she thought to herself and smiled. She felt good that he cared enough to get her out of harm's way.

"What they lookin' fo'?" Unc asked.

Hank responded by putting his hand up in the air like a pistol. Mystic smiled once again at the thought that whether they found a gun in his house or not, it wouldn't be the one he did the murder with."

"Anyway, he told us to come round here and get you Mystic. He told us to tell you to stand on the corner so he could at least see you," Toi said, waving for Mystic to follow them.

"Shit, I'm goin' too," Punkin chimed in, sliding her feet back in her flip flops.

"You know yo' big ass is one nosey muthafucka," Unc told Punkin.

"Shit nigga, don't act like you ain't gon' expect the 411 when I get back."

Unc chuckled.

"Shit, that's why I'm goin' too," he said, bouncing down the steps. "You know this my hood. I always gotta keep up with what's goin' down."

They all walked up Mimika and cut through the alley that led them to the side of Spider's house on Era. When they reached the end of the alley, Mystic's eyes searched the back of the police cruiser's for Spider's face. She found him sitting two cars back from where she was standing.

She couldn't see his face clearly because of the fence like cage in front of him. Punkin elbowed her and nodded across the street.

"Didn't I tell you they hoe's be jacked up?" Punkin chuckled. "That bitch look like she got Down Syndrome or somethin'. I hear the bitch can be ignorant too, so you might not wanna say too much to him unless you ready to get jiggy around this muthafucka."

Punkin looked down towards her feet.

"And tryin' to bang in flip flops ain't cool. I ain't tryin' to drag the skin off the top of my toes and shit."

Unc chuckled.

"Shit, it might help the appearance of them ugly muthafucka's."

"Fuck you, Unc," Punkin spit out.

Unc walked over and playfully hugged her.

"Aww baby, you know I'm playin'. You know you fine, from the ankles up!"

Punkin punched Unc in the arm.

Unc turned to Mystic and told her that he would go up to the car and holler at Spider for her as Mystic's eyes focused on the woman across the street. Unc approached the car, bent down to the window, talked for a moment and returned.

"They searchin' his crib fo' a gun like hank and 'nem said. He said some nigga round here snitchin' on him. But he told me to tell you he gon' call you when he get down to the station and to make sure you don't move his iron. Keep it safe."

Mystic shook her head so Spider would know she had gotten the message. She saw the wind blow out of him as he watched the detectives unload the packages of weed into an evidence bag.

119

They watched as the cars began to pull off one by one in front of them and the tow truck pulled up to tow the rental car for evidence.

"Damn, my shit in there," Mystic said,

"You can shit kiss goodbye fo' a minute cause they ain't gon' release that shit 'til after the trial," Unc told her.

As Spider passed her, he blew her a kiss. Mystic smiled at him and turned to walk away with Punkin and Unc. In the distance, you could hear his wife's voice.

"Im'a let his ass stay in there this time. Got these muthafucka's comin' up in my house; cuffin' me and shit. Fuck that nigga!"

Punkin slapped Mystic on the arm.

"Now that bitch know damn well she don't mean that shit. See that's what the fuck I'm talkin' 'bout."

"Yeah, cause as soon as he call her ass, she gon' jump to go get his ass and if she don't, if I was him, I'd beat her ass when I got out cause, bitch, how you gon' have all my money and leave me in jail," Unc added.

"I know that shit right," Punkin said, giving Unc a high-five.

Mystic was upset at the comments she heard his wife blaring all over the streets but at the same time, she saw it as an opportunity to move up to a new level in his life. She didn't know how she was gonna get him out but she knew in her heart, she would.

Chapter Nineteen

Tee-Tee awoke to the yelling of a voice screaming over the PA system, calling her cell block down to the cafeteria for chow. She rolled over on the concrete bunk and let her feet fall to the floor. She felt so dirty inside the dorm, filled with eighty to one hundred other women, from all walks of life. Some looking as if they had been there for years.

She just wanted to go home. Take a bath, comb her hair and brush her teeth. She knew her mom would be so upset if she found out where she'd been, so she decided to use her one phone call the night before, to call Big Slug.

When she told him what happened, he just chuckled in her ear.

"Funny how fucked up shit happens when you disobey me."

Tee-Tee rolled her eyes. This was not the time for him to trying to be Big Willie. She just wanted him to be around after her bond hearing so he could get her out. She knew he'd come because not only did he have her on the project concerning Cocamo but she also made a lot of money for him. It would be hustlin' suicide to leave her locked down.

"I may swing down there tomorrow. I got a lot of shit to do. Maybe some quiet time will put my muthafuckin' business back into perspective fo' you. I'll think about it."

With that he hung up the phone on his end and Tee-Tee hit the payphone with hers. She couldn't stand him. She hated the fact that she depended on him for her hustle.

His fat ass will be here. He just probably frontin' and stuntin' fo' some trick he layin' up with. Wanna her to think he

121

really got it like that. Big funky bastard! He scared to lay it down and do time fo' real. His fat will be here.

With that, she settled in the dorm and patiently waited for morning. She had sat down on the edge of her bunk and thought of Cocamo. She wondered what he was doing; wondered if he may possibly be thinking of her. Then she quickly chased the thought from her mind.

Shit, that nigga probably knee deep in pussy right now. That's all that nigga give a fuck about. How many bitches he can fuck.

Tee-Tee lined up for chow along the manila colored hallway. She made idle chit chat with her fellow inmates, devoured the doughy pancakes and half done sausage patty they were served for breakfast. The oatmeal was so thick, you could cement bricks with it. She was so ready to get out of there and she was so ecstatic when they returned to hear her name being called over the intercom to go across the street to satellite court.

Tee-Tee patiently waited for the small Pilipino female judge to set her bond. Twenty-five thousand, with ten percent cash or property. That meant she needed twenty-five hundred dollar to get out. She knew to Big Slug, that was chump change and so when she heard her name come blaring across the PA forty-five minutes later and she was told, "bag and baggage," she smiled to herself.

I knew it!

Although she wasn't in a big hurry to see Big Slug, knowing he would talk non-stop shit all the way back to the block, she was ready to get home to her family and friends. Her little girl, especially. The short time inside had allowed her reflect upon what little time she had been spending with her.

Tee-Tee wasn't proud of the mother she had become but she just kept telling herself that the things she could provide for her daughter, though the grind, outweighed the lack of bonding time she was able to spend with her. In Tee-Tee's mind, she was doing what was best for her baby girl.

Tee-Tee now stood at the discharge window, retrieving her personal belongings from an envelope the clerk had handed her. She put her earrings back in her ear, returned her gold chains to her neck and put her watch back onto her wrist. She put her ID into her back pocket and waited impatiently for the guard to release her.

When guard buzzed the steel, sliding door and it came to a closed behind her, Tee-Tee scanned the waiting room. She almost fainted when her eyes fell on the familiar face from the hood. Big Slug was no where to be found but there stood Cocamo by the door, staring out at the downtown traffic.

She was virtually paralyzed when she saw him.

I know this nigga ain't the one who bailed me out? How the fuck did he even know I was in here? Lil Curtis loose mouth ass! Nigga's mouth is just like a broken toilet, it runs all day and muthafuckin' night.

She exhaled a deep breath and began walking towards him. When he turned and saw her, he had to swallow the lump building inside his throat. The closer she came to him, the more he seemed to get choked up on the inside. He had to shake it off; regain his composure and quick. So when she finally stood before him, he used his best defense mechanism… being an asshole.

"Damn! You look a hot mess! I know they gave you one of them lil' jail packs and shit with the lil' black plastic comb in it. Maybe not cause you lookin' like a real tack head right about now."

123

"Very muthafuckin' funny nigga," Tee-Tee said, walking past him out the door. "What you doing down here anyway?"

He chirped the locks on the jeep and walked around to the driver's side to get in. Tee-Tee climbed into the passenger seat and Cocamo pulled off. It wasn't until they reached the McDonalds' drive thru on Tucker Blvd., that he finally opened his mouth.

"You hungry? I know that bologna sandwich and apple they gave you ain't fill you up."

"Naw, I'm good. I'll eat when I get home."

Cocamo sat back in his seat, staring at the menu.

"Aight but this ain't time to be full of all that pride and shit. Cause that shit ain't gon' keep yo' muthafuckin' stomach from growlin'."

"It ain't about no pride. I just said I'll eat when I get home. And again, what you doin' down here anyway? How you know where I was and why *you* of all people come get me out? What you got up yo' sleeve, nigga? I know…"

Cocamo held up his hand to quiet her.

"Damn! Can I order my damn food?"

He placed his order for a double cheeseburger meal and Tee-Tee just stared off out the window. She would never admit it out loud but it really had touched her in ways unimaginable that he had come to bond her out. She didn't know what his angle was but she was so sure he had one. Nigga's like Cocamo didn't do things like that just to be sweet. He wanted something and she was determined to find out what it was. She had no idea, that what he wanted, was simply… her.

Chapter Twenty

Unc knocked on Punkin's front door, with his black cordless phone in his hand.

"Aey, tell Mystic Spider's on the phone fo' her. He couldn't call her cell phone collect, so he called over to the house," he said, stepping inside the front door.

Punkin handed Unc the blunt in her hand, as she opened the basement door and yelled down for Mystic to come upstairs and get the phone. When Mystic reached the steps and heard who it was on the other end, her heart leaped with joy. She grabbed the phone from Unc and ran into the living room. Unc looked at her and laughed.

"Damn, he must've blew all up in between her ass. She grabbed that phone faster than a starvin' nigga, reachin' fo' the last piece of chicken."

Mystic plopped down onto the grey and black stripped couch, as his voice gleamed through the receiver.

"You aight?"

"Yeah, I'm good fo' now," Spider told her, leaning up against the off-white, concrete wall of his holding call, at the Justice Center downtown.

"This is my one phone call baby girl, so let's get everything accomplished we can."

Wow, one phone call and he chose me to call?

Mystic knew she was right, this was her time to shine and she was determined to take full advantage of it.

"I'm listening baby, what you need me to do?"

"Well first of all, they got all my tennis shoes and shit out the car, so I lost all my important shit, you feel me?"

Mystic knew that by *Tennis shoes*, he meant, all of his weed.

"It ain't like I got the receipt and can take that shit back to the store, you feel me? That's just bread I lost. But my nigga, Perez got some paper of mine, although I don't think its gon' be enough to buy me a new wardrobe. But it can get me some help to get up outta here. I need you to connect with him and grab that from him. Look up this Jew named Steinmyer in the phone book and go holla at him. See if he can be at my arraignment on Monday. That gives you four days to handle business, Boo, can you do that fo' me?"

Mystic didn't hesitate.

"Of course I can. I'll get on it as soon as I hang up the phone. What about that other news, I mean, why you?"

"Same shit, different day, mommy. They ain't got nothin' connectin' me to shit. But I feel like some muthafucka been runnin' they mouth. But all they could do is question me on the "hear say." But they found this shit in the process of comin' to me about that bullshit."

"So basically, we just gotta worry about the shoes you lost?"

"You got it but fuck all that at the moment. I'm standing in here with a room full of nigga's with hard dicks. Tell me something good to hold me over, 'til I hear yo' voice again," he told her.

Mystic lay back on the couch and reminisced about the previous night they'd spent together.

"You were so angry last night. I felt it in every thrust. Every time you plunged inside me, I could feel your rage. It felt as if you were trying to dig a tunnel to my heart. It felt so fuckin' good; the pain and the pleasure."

She paused.

"I really like the way you talked to me while you fucked me. The interaction shows me you were into it as much as I was. You made the word "bitch" sound so muthafuckin' sexy in the heat of passion."

"Is that right," he asked. "Damn mommy, I said tell me somethin' good, not somethin' that was gon' make my dick hard. I don't want no nigga up in here thinkin' they can test me cause, I'll never get out this muthafucka."

Mystic laughed.

"I'm just keepin' it gutta," she replied.

"And I like that in you. I got you when I come home. I got somethin' special fo' you."

"And what is that?"

"You'll see but you gotta handle that business fo' me first. My time is up, so I'ma clear this line. Look fo' my call tomorrow, about this time. You gotta work tonight, right?

"Yeah."

"Call my nigga and get on that befo' you go, aight? His number, 368-9588. And tell that nigga I said, pick you up from work. You know, I don't want you on that bus."

"Aight."

"Kiss me," he told her.

Without hesitation, she blew him a kiss through the receiver. When the line went dead, Mystic felt her heart getting heavy. Mystic looked at the number she'd scribbled on the paper. She dialed the number and waited for Perez to pick up on the other end of the line.

When he answered, Mystic got a little nervous about speaking with him over the phone. She was aware of the uncomfortable looks and stares she received from him. He always looked as if he was having *eye-gasms* when he saw her.

He would never vocalize his thoughts but she knew he often undressed her with his eyes. But now, she had to put all that aside and focus on Spider's money. She wouldn't however, ask him to take her to work as Spider commanded her to do because she really didn't want to be alone with him.

"Hey Perez, it's Mystic. I don't know if you heard what went down with Spider yet; but I just hung up talkin' to him and he asked me to call you."

"Yeah, I got word from his people. I got half of that but it's gon' take me a minute to get the rest. I'll get that to you when I pick you up from work later on."

"How'd you…"

"I'll be there 'round eleven."

Mystic sneered when he hung up the phone. It was something about Perez that just didn't sit right with her and sure shit, she was about to find out what it was.

Chapter Twenty One

Cocamo hadn't said another word to Tee-Tee until he had finished his meal. They were now exiting Hwy 70, onto Riverview Blvd. Cocamo brought the car to a stop just past Lillian in front of Northwest High School.

He placed his empty boxes in the bag, excited the jeep and walked over to the trash can. After he discarded them, he walked over to the blue painted, wooden bleachers and took a seat. He chuckled at the thought of her facial expressions back in the car.

He hadn't said much to her because he wasn't very good at expressing what he felt. He didn't know how to open up and let her inside his world. He was glad to see her but he couldn't even bring himself to say that to her either. Emotions just weren't his thing and as Tee-Tee came storming up beside him, him letting down his guard wouldn't happen anytime soon.

"Damn nigga, how the fuck you gon' just leave a bitch in the car while you over here chillin' and shit? That was some of the rudest shit I've ever seen. Like I ain't got shit to do? I been in jail all night. I'm tryin' to get home to see my baby girl and let my momma know I'm good and you actin' like a typical..."

"Do you ever shut the fuck up? I just laid down twenty-five hundred to get *yo'* ass outta jail and you can't even cut the *gangsta bitch* mentality long enough to say a simple, thank you? I didn't see nobody else's ass down there tryin' to bond yo' ass out," he said, taking a swallow of his Sprite soda.

"And why did you show up?" Tee-Tee asked, placing her hands on her hip. "I asked you before, what's yo' angle?"

She was starting to piss him off but he was trying to keep his cool.

"It's simple... money! I'm a business man. I saw an opportunity to make a lil' cash and I jumped on it," he lied.

"I put up twenty-five; you'll pay me back thirty-five."

"Thirty-five? Damn nigga, dat's a gee interest."

Cocamo sucked his teeth and smirked.

"Again, I didn't see no other muthafucka tryin' to get you outta there. And while you sittin' here tryin' to play baby gangsta with me, you need to go check that fat muthafucka that was gon' let yo' ass rot up in there."

He was trying to get her to see that working for Big Slug was getting her no where for real. It was petty money and didn't deserve the grind and sacrifices she made to make another nigga rich.

Tee-Tee looked off towards the street.

"Yeah, that's what I thought! You can't go at him with all this bull shit but you'll come at me like I'm one of yo' lil' flunkies on the block. So again, I'ma need that thirty-five up out you. And you got thirty days to deliver."

He rose up from the bleachers, stepped down and walked behind her. He popped her on the ass.

"It's business baby, never personal."

With that he walked back to the jeep and got inside. He knew she was boiling inside but he also knew she couldn't do anything but respect what he'd said. He didn't care how it made her feel. After everything he had gone through the previous night; going back and forth in his mind concerning what he should do about getting her out, he didn't appreciate the attitude Tee-Tee was giving him.

I knew I should've have gone outta my way to help this bitch! This shit ain't me, I'm trippin'!"

Tee-Tee however, had gotten the message, loud and clear. She knew she was being ungrateful for all he had done for her. Just like Cocamo, Tee-Tee didn't know how to accept help. It made her feel weak and vulnerable in some way. Had Big Slug gotten her out of jail, it wouldn't have been so serious to her because she understood that that was part of his job as being a boss in the game. With Cocamo, it felt different. Against Big Slug's orders, she had begun falling for him and she really felt bad for not being able to express it.

She also understood the game and couldn't be mad at the interest, knowing had it been Big Slug's money, it would be doubled. She walked over to the jeep, climbed inside and looked at the road up ahead.

Cocamo shook his head, put the jeep in drive and pulled off. Once they passed the Miami Grill at Theodore and Riverview, Tee-Tee turned to him.

"Coco, I really do appreciate you comin' down there to get me. You gotta unda'stand that I ain't use to that. I ain't use to nobody doin' anything fo' me without it being beneficial to them in some way."

"It is beneficial to me, business wise."

"Yeah, I know but I ain't mean it like that. I'm sayin'... well, just, thank you. And I will have yo' grip fo' you in thirty days. Less if I put in overtime."

Cocamo glanced over at her out the corner of his eye. He watched her, twiddling with her thumbs. It took a lot for her to say that to him, he knew. He also understood her feelings. She like him, was used to handling things on her own, making a way out of no way. It's hard to accept when someone comes at you and just wants to be apart of you life for no reason other than they just enjoy being around you.

When you're in the game, it's always people around you looking for what the can *take* from you, not give *to* you.

131

"It's all good, I know you got me and I know you appreciate the love… I mean, the helping hand. It's understandable that I'd be the last person you'd expect to see in that waiting room."

As the jeep headed up Harney to Mimika, a RAC (Random-Ass-Chick), came running towards the jeep, trying to get Cocamo's attention. When he stopped the jeep, the short light skinned woman leaned against his door.

"Hey baby, I'm tryin' to see if we can hook up later on?"

Tee-Tee snickered and shook her head. How could she ever bring herself to get serious about him. He, in her eyes, was such a whore.

Cocamo heard the snicker and chuckled himself. He knew what she was thinking but had she focused in on the woman, she would've known she was a clucka. Yet, he like the small show of jealousy she was displaying.

He told the woman to holla at him later and continued onto Tee-Tee-s house. When they reached the front, he looked over at her.

"Look I know you got business to handle but if you got time, get at me later."

"Damn, didn't you just tell that lil' ratchet ass bitch that a minute ago? You ain't doin' like that nigga. I'm good, I'ma go get this money."

He smiled to himself. Yes, she was jealous and it kinda touched him. She got out the jeep and headed up the steps to her front porch.

"Aey," he called after her. "She a clucka, she want some shit. Like I said, get at me."

With that, he drove off and Tee-Tee opened the front door. As soon as it closed behind her, her mother Yvette lit into her something terrible. Tee couldn't stand to hear it at the moment.

She walked over to the play pen, grabbed her daughter, went into her bedroom and slammed the door. Yvette banged on the door and continued to threaten Tee-Tee with calling CPS (Child Protective Services) on her, if she didn't get her act together.

Tee-Tee lay across the best, tuning out the screams of her mother and looked at her baby girl. She needed to get back out onto the block. She had a lot of money to make. Big Slug's, her own and now Cocamo's. As she rubbed her daughter's stomach, she prayed that one day the little girl would understand that Tee-Tee was only trying to do the best she could by her.

"It's hard out here lil' momma. Ain't nobody gon' give us nothin'. Momma in there talkin' all that shit but we'd all be in the streets if I didn't grind out here like I do. I'm doin' this alone. I ain't got nobody helpin' me."

With that, she thought of Cocamo.

Why did he feel the need to explain who that girl was? That was totally outta character for him.

She smiled to herself and grabbed her baby girl in her arms. She lay there, holding the most important person in her life and thinking of the one who was becoming the second, Cocamo.

Chapter Twenty Two

Mystic felt antsy and uncomfortable her entire shift at work. She was not looking forward to being alone in Perez's company. She hoped he had gotten busy and wouldn't show up but as she clocked out and walked outside the sliding door at the Walgreens; she realized she would have no such luck. The champagne colored, Cutlass, was waiting in the parking lot for her.

Perez saw Mystic exit the store and smirked to himself. He had lusted over her since he'd first laid eyes on her. He and Spider had engaged in many conversations concerning Mystic before Spider had actually said something to her the day Kay Kay had gotten shot.

Like Spider, Perez was married as well and also like Spider, Perez played around, constantly too. However, Perez was a different breed of cheaters. He liked his women young, almost child like. Most of them were between the ages of sixteen and twenty-one. He was viewed as a predator by most and as Mystic opened the passenger side door, the chill that blew down her spine, echoed those thoughts.

When she closed the door, she heard the locks pop immediately. Perez turned onto Halls Ferry and headed towards the Riverview Circle. He rounded the circle to Broadway and made a right.

"You hungry?" he asked her.

Mystic just wanted to hurry up and get out of the car with him, so she declined.

"Come on, it won't take but a second. I just wanna get a box of rice or somethin'."

Mystic, against her better judgment, nodded her head in agreement. Perez pulled over in front of the rice house and told Mystic to come inside.

"We can handle biz while we wait on the food."

Perez knew that Spider had Mystic so far underneath his thumb, he knew the only way he could get inside her panties or her mouth, was to tarnish the pedestal Mystic had put him on. He would worry about the repercussions with his long-time friend, later. He and Spider had never gone through changes over women. Most of the time, it was just some stray they may have picked up off the streets. They ran trains on chicken heads all the time in the hood.

It was never an issue of having sex with the same woman. They too, lived by the theory of *M.O.B.* Besides, deep inside Perez chuckled at the thought of Spider seriously steppin' to him.

That nigga wouldn't be shit without me, he thought to himself.

"So, what's the plan?" he asked Mystic, taking a seat across from her in the small orange booth.

"What do you mean, what's the plan? Spider needs his money so I can get him a lawyer. It's that simple."

"It's that simple, huh?" he smirked.

His eyes slid downward, towards her breast. He sucked his teeth and Mystic felt like she wanted to throw up.

"It's neva that simple when all you have is some of the money required to do what you need to do. He's gon' need way more than this to get out of the shit he's in. A lawyer may take this change I got, for a down payment but he's gon' want more, a lot more. And even if I get the rest of it, it won't be enough. So again, I ask you, what's yo' plan cause I know Walgreens ain't payin' you that much," he said nodding towards her name tag.

Mystic rolled her eyes and looked off to the wall. Perez was shady and she didn't know how much longer she could stand it.

Just gimme his fuckin' money and I'll walk home, bastard!

"I mean, ain't that what he got boys for? Can't you guys kick down the rest? I know he'd do the same for one of you."

Perez snickered as he turned back to check the window and see if his order was ready. He was ready to go. He had plans to use the present situation to his advantage.

"You right about that, lil lady. When you dealin' with 'hood love, you do *whatever* you gotta do to keep yo' peeps good."

Mystic definitely did not like the way he expressed that *whatever*. He leaned in closer to her.

"I know I got love fo' him, do you? And if so, how much? I mean…"

He grabbed her hand.

"…What would you do to get him home?"

Mystic jerked her hand away.

The short Chinese woman, called his order and Mystic felt so relived when he stood to retrieve it and answer his phone. She shook her head.

Nigga's ain't shit! I can't wait to tell him, his boy came at me.

Perez grabbed his order and they walked to the car. Mystic purposely falling behind him. She wanted as much distance a possible.

When they got back in the car, Perez sat his rice on the back seat, cut the radio on and looked over to Mystic, who was staring out the window.

"I gotta go pick the money up from my pat'na."

"What? You didn't bring it with you?" Mystic asked, irritated.

"Naw," he responded. "We don't ride like that. Shit that's an invitation to get robbed or hit up by them jump-out-boys. Just sit back and chill."

Perez cut the radio up and bumped, Jahiem's, **Hush.**

"*... I can not believe this, we just laid it down. What are you gonna tell him, when he comes back in town? Are you gonna let him know, that I'm givin' you the business? I try my best to let it go but I could not resist it. It's to temptin', I'm slippin', touchin' and feelin'. Me and him be kickin' it, while all the while I'm hittin' it, whooo...*"

Perez started snapping his fingers and bobbing his head to the music.

"Aww yeah, that's that shit there," he said. "Yeah, that's that gangsta shit."

Mystic caught the meaning in the words and rolled her eyes back in the top of her head.

Neva nigga will you touch this! She returned to staring out the window.

"*... I know that girl it's gonna be hard fo' me to run with him. Cause we be hoopin' and shit, that's my dog, my best friend. Said I'm never gonna let a trick come between me and my homie. Had a little to much drink and I let you put it on me...*"

Mystic had never been to Perez's house before with Spider but the current scenery suggested to her that he didn't live in O'Fallon Park. He pulled up behind a four door, white Chevy Blazer and cut off his headlights. It was dark and Mystic was getting more uncomfortable by the second.

The driver stepped out of the Blazer and Mystic relaxed a little once he approached the driver's side window and she could see his face. It was the same Indian looking guy that Spider had sold the weed to the first time he picked her up from work.

137

Mystic smiled as she thought back to that first night. He had made such good love to her that night. She missed him terribly and she promised herself that she would do whatever it took, to get him home.

The Indian gentleman placed a wad of cash in Perez's hand, chit-chatted for a minute and left. Mystic waited impatiently for Perez to start the car after the man had driven off but instead, he just leaned back in his seat and looked at Mystic.

"So, what is it you see in that nigga anyway? I mean, that's my boy, don't get me wrong but what is it somebody like you really see in a nigga like that?"

Mystic was getting upset very quickly. This was supposed to be his boy and here he was, trying to down him to his woman. Mystic wanted to spit in his face but she needed to get Spider's money. She decided it would be better if she just went along with his game.

"I don't know what you mean by that question. Why would you say, a nigga like that? A nigga like what? And if he's such a wanksta, why do *you* hang out with him? I'm with him because to me, he got it goin' on. He's gangsta…that's my thug-a-boo!"

Perez burst out laughing and hit the steering wheel for emphasis.

"Gangsta? Thug-a-what? You sound like a groupie or somethin'. Listen at yo'self. You need somebody that's gon' lace you with the finer things, put you up in a place of yo' own, get you a whip… fuck a bus! Shit like that! So you've gon' coo-coo for coco puffs, over a nigga with a few pennies? Wow, I'da got a shot at that first, if I knew it would be that easy."

"Easy? Who you callin' easy? Look Perez, can I just have his money so I can go? I'll walk home. I don't need you to take me no where!"

Mystic held her hand out and waited for Perez to give her Spider's money but instead, Perez let his seat back even further and chuckled to himself. He admired her spunk and loyalty. He wanted it for himself but if he couldn't have it, he would attempt to get something out the deal. He un-fastened his belt buckle, un-zipped his pants and pulled out his jimmy. He started stroking it while he stared at Mystic. He was jacking if off, right there in front of her.

Mystic's stomach turned at the sight of the limp, spaghetti noodle in front of her. She wanted no parts of it or him. She grabbed her purse and reached over to unlock the door.

"You need his money, right? How bad you want him home? Put yo' mouth on it. Show me how bad you want him home. Do this fo' me and I'll make sure I get you the rest of the money you need."

Mystic felt her eyes begin to well up with tears. How bad did she want him home? And how could his boy even ask such bullshit of her? Mystic closed her eyes and saw his face. She really did want to bring him home and she did promise herself she'd do anything. She opened her eyes and saw Perez looking as if he was about have a seizure.

Maybe it won't take that long, she reasoned with herself.

She leaned down towards his lap, closed her eyes and almost threw up.

Chapter Twenty Three

Tee-Tee looked down at the number vibrating across her phone. She had avoided answering his call all day.

Now the fat muthafucka got time fo' me. When I was sittin' in that hell hole, he wasn't fuckin' wit' me. Now he know I'm here bout to get my grind on and he wanna be a bug-a-boo.

She was crossing the street at Floy when Big Slug pulled away from the curb at Mimika and West Florissant. He had been watching her for about an hour and calling her to see if she was going to answer his call. The fact that she hadn't had now pissed him off and he was ready to take it out on her.

He swirled the Suburban directly in her path and by the time Tee-Tee could react, he had damn near knocked her off her feet. He brought the truck to a halt and jumped out with his .38 aimed at her.

"So this how we playin' it now? Didn't I tell you, you don't run shit in my muthafuckin' streets? I sat down at the end of the block and watched you check my call three muthafuckin' times. I been near, so I know you ain't doin' business like that. So why don't you gimme one good reason not to smoke yo' ass fo' not answerin' my muthafuckin' call. Is it cause that nigga bailed you outta jail?"

Tee-Tee eyes got wide.

How on earth did he know that?

"Yeah, I came down there to get yo' ass out so you could make my money. But when I got there I saw yo' boy postin' yo' bond so I laid back and let him handle it. I thought about it fo' a minute. I said to myself, damn, she must be handlin' her business after all if she got this nigga bondin' her out and shit. Which means…"

He walked up close to her and pointed the gun at her head. Lil' Curtis and Harvey watched in horror, knowing what type of man Big Slug was.

"Come on Slug man, you ain't even gotta handle this shit like this," Lil' Curtis told him, stepping out into the street.

Big Slug turned to him and aimed the gun at Lil' Curtis.

"You want some of this nigga? Huh? You betta take yo' ass back up on that raggedy ass porch fo' I lay yo' bitch ass down right beside her."

Lil' Curtis looked to Tee-Tee and held up his hands.

"Look here man, I ain't tryin' to do all that wit' you. Them my people. She ain't tryin' to cross you or nothin' like that I'm just sayin.."

Big Slug cocked his gun.

"I'm just sayin', shut the fuck up and stay out my muthafuckin' business!"

"So sad," Lil Curtis said, looking to Tee-Tee once again. "Umm, I'ma just wait fo' you over there," he said, pointing to the porch.

Lil' Curtis walked over to the bottom of his house steps and joined Harvey.

"Man, this nigga here crazy," Harvey said, patting Lil Curtis on the chest.

"Shit, dat nigga just mad cause he hungry."

Tee-Tee looked up at the corner of Mimika and Shulte.

Damn, why he can't drive down the street right now? I know if he'd cared enough to get me out of jail, he wouldn't let this just kill me in front of him.

"So since you got this nigga willin' to put up money fo' you and shit, I'ma assume you close enough to this nigga to handle yo' business. Shit and you got the best of both worlds.

You got this nigga's money on yo' bond ticket and when take him out, you get to eat like we should be eatin'. It's a win-win situation."

He walked up within inches from her face, placed the barrel of the gun firmly underneath her chin and spoke where only she could hear him. Tee-Tee thought she'd wet herself. She had no choice but look at him, directly in his eyes. He applied more pressure.

"I'd betta hear it on the news tonight or yo' peoples will be hearin' bout you on tomorrow's. Am I makin' myself clear?"

Tee-Tee took a hard swallow of her saliva.

"Yeah, you clear," she said, a single tear rolling down her face.

He backed up, placed his gun back in the front of his waist and started laughing. He brushed off Tee-Tee's shoulders.

"Shake it off baby. I told you, it's all about loyalty."

He turned away and began walking towards. She pictured herself, stabbing him over and over again. He looked over to Lil Curtis and Harvey. He made the symbol of a gun with his index finger and thumb. He gave them a wink.

"You nigga's stay up and watch yo' backs out here, it's ugly."

He jumped in the Suburban and drove off. Tee-Tee crossed the street and went onto the steps with her crew.

"You should've let some rounds off in that fat ass nigga. We need some chitlin's round this muthafucka fo' Thanksgiving. Fat ass!"

"I ain't got my strap, nigga, you do! I left it over here, remember? *You* shoulda popped his fat ass. Where my shit at anyway?" she asked, wiping her face.

"Yo' boy got it. I took all yo' shit up there to him when you got locked up."

Okay, so that's why he told me to holla at him. If I wasn't so busy cussin' him out, he might've told me he had my shit.

Tee-Tee looked up at Lil' Curtis.

"Yeah well, he won't catch me out here again like that. I'll be back."

She walked up Mimika and landed on Cocamo's door step. She knocked on the door. Unc answered and told her that Cocamo wasn't there. He told her that he'd be back shortly and that she was more than welcome to come inside and wait for him.

Tee-Tee knew Cocamo would flip out if he walked in the door and found her sitting there. He had expressed to her on more than one occasion that his pest peeve was people showing up at his house, unannounced. But this was important. She needed to get her gun from him, either to protect herself from Big Slug or to carry out his orders and kill Cocamo.

143

Chapter Twenty Four

Mystic ran down to the Amoco Gas Station on the corner of West Florissant and Warne Avenue. She had jumped out of the car while Perez still had his jimmy in his hand. She wouldn't...she couldn't. She would just have to figure out another way to get the money for Spider's bail because she refused to put her mouth on Perez or anyone else for that matter.

She pulled out her cell phone and called Breeze.

"Is Man by you? I need a ride home."

"Naw, hit him on his cell. Where you at?"

"The Amoco by O'Fallon Park."

"What the hell you doin over there this time of night? You got a death wish or somethin'? Girl you better hop the first muthafuckin' thing smokin'. If Man don't answer, get the bus or call a cab. But you need to get the fuck from over them ways," Breeze told her.

She hung up the phone as the Cutlass pulled up along side of her.

"Get in the car, it was just a test. I was just testin' you to see if you really had my nigga's back or not," he lied.

"Naw, that wasn't no muthafuckin' test! If I would've put my lips on yo' dick, you damn sure wasn't gon' say, get up; Testin' me? Nigga, please!"

"Fine then, walk home. But don't let me hear this shit in the streets, you feel me? Trust me when I say you don't wanna start a war out here between fam. You chose not to get down, leave it at that. You wanna walk, walk. But you better learn the rules of the game and quick. Now here bitch, get this money."

He held out a brown paper bag through the window. Mystic stopped walking, stared at the bag for a minute and decided that she'd better take it, right there, out in the open. She walked over to the car and grabbed to bag. She noticed the white, sticky cream on the bag and her hand.

"What the..." she said, looking at her hand.

"Oh yeah, that's the one that was meant fo' you to swallow," he said, chuckling.

"Remember what I said, don't let me hear in the streets or else," he told her, patting his hand on his pistol, laying on his lap.

Mystic shook her head. She knew nothing about the street game for real and the last thing she wanted to do was come up missing. She just wanted to get her man out of jail. Now that she had the money in her hand, it was no need, she decided, to take what had just happened in the park, any further.

"You won't," she told him. "Thanks for the money."

He let up the window to the passenger side door and slowly sped away. Mystic searched through her phone for Man's number. She was really scared to be out with all that money in her pocket. Especially since she had no idea that Perez had pulled over at the and called a couple of his little thunder cats and told them that, he had just given Mystic three grand and she was alone standing at the gas station. He wanted it back from her and he wanted them to get it for him. They agreed.

When Mystic heard Man's call tone, she anxiously awaited for him to pick up the phone.

"..one more chance, Biggie give me one more chance. First things first, I Poppa freaks all the honeys, dummies, playboy bunnies, those wantin' monies..."

"Yeah?" he answered.

"Man, this is Mystic. I was wondering if you could come and get me. I'm Amoco by O'Fallon Park."

"Yeah, I ain't that far from you. What you doin' that way anyway?"

"Long story, my ride from work went sour. Are you comin' now? I got a lot of money on me and I'm scared," she told him.

Man was over a chick's house getting the same service that Perez had asked of Mystic. The only difference was that, this chick was a more-than-willing participant.

When Mystic told him she had a lot of cash on her and where she was located, he jumped to go and pick her up. He told the chick he had to make a run and she'd have to wait for another time to finish her mission.

The chick didn't like this. She wanted what she wanted and she was determined to get it. As Man tried to pull away from her, She responded with a force that he could not fight. A force that demanded him to surrender to her will and he did. Within seconds, she had the protein shake she was looking for and Man had the trembles.

He stumbled to his feet, fixed his clothes and grabbed his keys. He looked over to the chick and shook his head.

Damn, them muthafuckas' oughta be in the SuperHead hall –of-fame!

His thoughts were interrupted by the vibration on his hip. He checked his cell phone. It was Mystic, again.

"I'm three minutes from you baby, I'll be at you in just a few minutes, aight?

Mystic paced on the other end of the line as she continued to notice some of the characters patronizing the Amoco.

"Can you hurry? It's some crazy lookin' nigga's walkin' towards me."

"Stay cool, I'm on my way."

146

Man hung up the phone and hit the gas. He liked Mystic, liked her spirit. He didn't think she belonged in the hood and all its drama. He didn't like her dealing with Spider, either. Man had known Spider a long time from the hood and he'd seen first hand how Spider treated the women in his life. Women he claimed he cared about. Man felt Spider would get her into something that would get her hurt or worse; he was right.

The two young misfits were approaching her location, planning their attack along the way. Perez had instructed them to make it look like a real robbery, rough her up a little but don't kill her. As they neared her, Mystic clutched her purse and began to walk closer to the gas station window. It was the most well lit area. But as her pace increased, so did theirs.

One of the young men began to call after her.

"Aey, aey... do you got change fo' a ten, so me and my boy can catch the bus?"

Mystic didn't respond, she just kept walking, wishing Man would hurry up. The other young boy that was with him, ran up to Mystic and passed her. He acted as if he was simply running ahead to the gas station but he turned abruptly and was blocking her path.

"Aey Bitch, you heard him! You got change fo'a ten or not?"

Mystic looked around to see how much further she had to go before reaching the window. Realizing that she still had a distance to go, she decided to answer his question.

"Please, I don't have any change. I'm waiting fo' a ride home myself. I just wanna get to the window," she told him, stepping to her right to walk around him.

He put his hand up on her shoulder to stop her.

"No change, huh? I think you lyin'," he said looking at his counter part, who was now directly behind Mystic.

147

"I think the bitch is lyin' cuz, how 'bout you?"

She heard the knife click her ear and she almost fainted. The boy behind her pressed it against the lobe of her right ear. Mystic kept her eyes on the tattoo underneath the left eye of the robber in front of her. It was the tattoo of a cross.

"The purse or yo' life bitch!"

The second click came, much louder than the first one and it startled them all. Mystic could tell by the look on the young thief's face in front of her, the click didn't come at the hands of his accomplice.

"Tell daddy how you want it?"

Mystic knew the voice all to well. It was Man. Her heart felt such relief as she watched the one in front of her take off running down the street, towards Grand Avenue.

"That's ya boy, huh? You see he left yo' punk ass here by yo'self, huh?"

Man told Mystic to get in the car. Mystic ran across the Amoco parking lot, jumped into Man's jeep and locked the door. Her hands were shaking she was so terrified. She put her hand over her heart and tried to calm herself down. She had never experienced anything like that in her life before. She looked out the window and watched as Man pistol whipped the dusty boy until he lay damn near, life-less on the ground.

He added a couple of kicks to make a statement before coming back to the jeep. Mystic popped the lock to let him inside. He floored it onto West Florissant, heading back towards the hood.

"Thank you Man, thank you so much for coming when you did," Mystic told him, as her eyes began to water.

Man grabbed her hand.

"It's all good, Mimi, you know I ain't gon' let nobody fuck with you. You just like my lil sister. I'll hurt a nigga over you, you see that."

Mystic nodded her head.

"What was you doin' out here this time of night, in this neck of the woods?"

Mystic wiped her face and began to tell Man the entire events from that night, from start to finish.

"That's a hoe ass nigga fo' even sending you to that nigga to make that transaction. You don't put yo' girl in harms way like that. He know them nigga ain't shit. Why he didn't send one of them rats from the block he be fuckin' with? I got a good mind to beat his ass when he get outta there."

Mystic tried to defend her man.

"I don't think he trusted any of them to do what he needed them to do. He knew I would use the money to handle his business."

"Yeah? Look at what handlin' his muthafuckin' business almost got you. Mystic these streets ain't nothin' to play with. You can not be out here in these streets if the street ain't in you. It's one thing to be book smart but bein' street smart is something altogether different. Them nigga's would've killed you without a second thought, you feel me? You had no muthafuckin' business out there!"

Mystic tears began to flow harder at the elevation in Man's voice. He pulled over in front of the Calvary cemetery at Kingshighway and West Florissant. He wiped the tears from her cheeks.

"Look, Mimi, I'm sorry. I didn't mean to yell at you like that. This whole shit with my lil cuz getting' killed, is fuckin' with me. He lost his life over some stupid shit. Being in somethin' that didn't have nothin' to do with him. In the wrong shit at the right time. That was you, a minute ago.

You know that lil' nigga was more than just my cousin. I raised him in this business and he prospered to the point that I made him my right hand man," he said, taking a swallow of his liquor.

"His only problem was he was too flashy. I always tried to tell him that shit. Stuntin' ain't where it's at all the time. It's just a road to the Feds or the grave. You can only survive in this game when you don't make a lot of noise. I tried to tell him…bad boys, real bad boys move in silence."

He went on to speak of the crazy times he and his cousin has shared together but when he spoke of their true closeness, a closeness of more than just cousins but more like brother's. He pounded his fist against the steering wheel and took a hard swallow of his Remy. He began driving again.

"Look Mimi, all I'm sayin' is, I know you feelin' this nigga and all but let me ask you this… why you think he didn't send his muthafuckin' wife to handle this shit for him? Why didn't he put her in jeopardy? He knew she wasn't fuckin' with him like that. Bein' top bitch don't mean, get yo'self killed," he said, pulling up to grab a pack a Newport's, from the Phillip 66 at Park Lane.

"When a man knows he's got a diamond, he does everything and anything to protect it and make sure it always shines. And if the nigga never takes care of it, it will eventually dull and then the nigga don't want it no more. He'll go out and get a new one, feel me?"

Again, Mystic nodded her head in agreement.

"All I'm sayin' Mimi, is… make sure you can handle the game *before* you remove the plastic and break out the dice. Cause the game is like shootin' craps, you gotta be willing to lose what's valuable to you, even if that's yo' life."

Mystic turned to look out the window.

"Nobody needs to know what happened tonight. This will stay 'tween us. When that nigga call you tomorrow, you tell him you got his money and that's where yo' part of this shit stops, you hear me? Tell him, he's gotta come up with the rest another way, a way that *don't* involve you."

Mystic exhaled a long sigh as the Jeep pulled onto Mimika and stopped in front of the house. Man leaned over and gave her a kiss on her cheek.

"Gon' in the house Mimi and don't let nobody know you got that dough on you. Don't worry about that snake ass nigga Perez neither, I got him."

Mystic did as Man said without another word. She got half way up the steps and turned back to watch him pull away. When he disappeared over the hill, Mystic sat down on the ledge of the porch and started thinking.

I know he saved my life but he's wrong about Spider. I know he loves me and that's why he chose me to help him. So he can come home to me. Man don't understand. Nobody does; if I show him I can be by his side thru thick and thin, maybe, just maybe I'll finally be somebody's diamond.

Mystic went inside, slipped past Punkin's room and headed down stairs. She flopped down on the bed and began to lay out her plan. A plan that would prove to everybody that she indeed, could handle the street life and the game.

Chapter Twenty Five

Cocamo pulled up to the house to find Tee-Tee sitting on the steps, waiting for him. He tilted his head and looked over at the girl in his passenger seat. He had so many plans for her that evening. He'd just left his homeboy Vice's house and hooked up with the light skinned, thick framed female. Tee-Tee was threatening to put a damper on his party.

"Hol' up, I'll be right back."

He got out the car and walked up to the steps. Tee-Tee looked up at him and held up her hands before he could open his mouth and say something crazy.

"I know, I came unannounced. I really need to get my strap from you and I'm on my way. You can go on wit' yo' night."

Cocamo looked at her, then to the female waiting for him in his car. Tee-Tee looked around him to the car. It bothered her to see the girl but she had more pressing things on her mind at the time. She had no time to get into anything with him. Besides, what could she really say? She wasn't his woman and he made it clear on several occasions that their relationship was based on pure sex and now that he'd bonded her out, business.

She stood up on the step, brushed off the back of her jeans and asked him if she could just come inside and get what she needed. Cocamo said *yes* and opened the door to let her inside. He went into his room, retrieved the shoe box from his closest and headed back into the living room.

He handed her the purse with her gun inside. Tee-Tee thanked him and walked out the door. He knew something was wrong with her cause that was to easy. She was preoccupied with something serious because he knew, with the flip mouth she had, she would've said something about the female in his jeep.

He walked outside onto the porch and watched as she disappeared down Harney. He then looked over to the jeep at the fine female waving at him and told her to get out the car. He did exactly what Tee-Tee told him to do, he went on with his night. When she reached the porch, he opened the door for her to go inside.

He told her to have a seat on the couch and asked her if she wanted anything to drink.

"Oh no, I don't drink," she said, looking around the living room.

He went into his bedroom to get the blunt out of his weed tray. He returned to the living room and attempted to hand it to her.

"You wanna fire up?"

"I don't smoke either."

Cocamo snickered and walked over to the stereo. He turned on Majic 104.9 and went into the kitchen. He reached in the cabinet, got a glass and poured him a drink of Remy. He gulped down a mouth full.

That's what I get fo' tryin' to fuck a county bitch!

He walked back into the living room and turned up the volume on the radio. Instantly, she held up her hand and gestured for him to turn it down.

"Little too loud, don't you think?" she asked him, covering her ears.

Cocamo turned down the stereo and exhaled a deep breath. He took a seat beside her.

"Okay so, you don't drink, you don't smoke; don't like loud music… what else do you *not* do?"

She laughed and hit him on the arm, playfully. Then she began telling him everything he really didn't want to hear. All about her life in the suburbs and how spoiled she was. She talked about how she expected her man to take care of her and spend all his money on making her happy.

Im'a kill that nigga Vice, he thought to himself, as he inhaled his blunt.

The song on the radio caught his attention, the words forcing him to tune out everything she was saying. And focus on the lyrics.

"...If I would've knew the girl next door would've been you, I would've been nice to you, A little more kind to you, I would've looked twice at you. If I would've knew the girl next door would've been you, I probably would've shared my grub, depending on how close we was, by now we would be so in love..."

Cocamo stared off into space and thought back to the look Tee-Tee had on her face when she left.

What if she was really in some kind of trouble, he thought to himself.

He didn't want anything happening to her. He had to protect his investment, he reasoned. He couldn't bring himself to admit that it was much more than that. He wanted, no he *needed* to make sure she was okay.

He looked at the female sitting beside him, mouth still moving non-stop and he held up his hand to quiet her. She snapped her neck to the side in disbelief and gave him an, *"I know you didn't just shush me,"* look.

"I gotta go. I gotta go check on my peoples."

He grabbed his keys and stood up at the door. He swung the door open, remembering his strap in the bedroom, underneath his mattress. He went and retrieved his gun, came back into the living room and told her, "let's go."

The female rolled her eyes, uncrossed her legs, grabbed her purse and stormed out the door. Cocamo chuckled to himself.

"This here bitch crazy."

He locked the door behind him and jumped in the jeep. Her face was all tore up and she spent the ride home, talking on her cell phone, telling the caller what a terrible time she had. When he reached her house in Ferguson, she got out the jeep, closed the door and leaned into the passenger window.

"Umm, I don't think it's a good idea for you to call me. I don't think we're gonna be a good fit for each other."

Cocamo took a hit off his blunt, held the smoke for a second and exhaled it directly in her face.

"I think you right. You too muthafuckin' stuck up fo' me."

He threw the jeep in reverse and floored the petal with her still hanging in the window. The jerk caused her to fall, face first on the ground. Cocamo kept driving, laughing at the belligerent comments she made as she stood to her feet and began dusting off her clothes. She didn't matter to him anyway. He had his mind set on other business and that business was finding Tee-Tee.

Chapter Twenty Six

Mystic awoke to Punkin, tapping on her leg and handing her the telephone.

"It's Spider," Punkin said. "And tell him, he my nigga and all but *damn* on the collect calls!"

Mystic sat up in the bed, looked down at the receiver and thought about what Man had told her the previous night. There was no need to bring up anything that had happened the night before because it could only hurt her creditability, not help it. So Mystic tossed the events of yesterday to the back of her mind and said hello to her man.

"Hey Momma, how'd you sleep?"

Mystic looked off to the wall and exhaled. She really did miss him.

How come, just when I find what I'm lookin' for, he gotta go and get locked up?

"I slept okay I guess but that's only cause you weren't here to tuck me in."

"I like that in you, Ma. So, did Perez kick you down last night?"

The thought alone of him, made her sick to her stomach. Mystic wanted so badly to tell him everything Perez had said and done but she didn't want any further back lash from Perez. He would get his sooner or later; Man had promised her so.

"Yeah I got it. It was only half of what he owed you though. He said it would take him a few days before he could get the rest. But he did tell me to ask you for Remo's number for him," she lied.

She lay in her bed the night before and thought of a way to double, maybe even triple the money Perez had given her. She figured, if she hooked up with Remo, buy a few zips from him, she could ask Man to do his thang and make it pop.

"He said he might have to make moves, if you need more than what he can get his hands on right now."

Spider, without hesitation, gave Mystic Remo's cell phone number and told her to get back up with Perez. He had a bail hearing in three days. Mystic rolled her eyes on the other end of the phone. There was no way she was calling Perez for shit else. She would do this on her own, her way. But to keep him calm, she lied and promised him she would.

When Spider hung up the line, Mystic placed the call to Remo and explained to him what was going on. Remo without hesitation, told her to come on up to Indy. He told her he'd take real good care of her. Mystic, despite the slithering sound in his voice, hung up the phone and made plans to leave that afternoon. She called her job first, called off and went next door to Breeze's room.

She wanted to ask Breeze if she would tag along to Indy but when Breeze opened the door, Mystic quickly got second thoughts. Breeze was in the game, true, but she was also under Man's thumb and couldn't hold water when it came to keeping anything from him.

So when Breeze asked her what was up, Mystic asked to borrow some hair gel and returned to her room. She got out the phone book and called Greyhound. The bus ride to Indy would only be a few hours. If she left at Noon, she could be in Indy by four o'clock that afternoon. Then she could catch the outgoing bus at seven o'clock and be back home by Midnight.

No one would suspect a thing because Mystic was always at work until that time anyway. She grabbed her duffel bag, filled it with some clothes, zipped up the bag and put it in a trash bag like she was going outside to empty the garbage. She stashed the bag on the side of the raggedy white garage and went back inside to get ready.

Mystic threw on a pair of blue jeans and a t-shirt Spider had bought her that last time they were in Indy. She pulled her hair in a ponytail and walked upstairs.

The porch was crowded with the usual gang, sitting back, smoking blunts and discussing all the neighborhood gossip. Mystic walked outside and waved *hello* to everyone on the porch. She had no time to stop and talk. The bus left in an hour. Mystic had to come up with an excuse on where she was heading.

"Whad-dup, neicy?" Unc asked her, giving her a hug. "You good?"

Mystic smiled at him.

"I'm good, Unc, how 'bout you?"

"I bet you are now that you done talked to that nigga," Fred said.

"Whatever Fred," she responded.

"You need to quit playing and let me gon' on and hit that. Cause I know that nigga, ain't tappin' that pussy right."

Fred had been trying to get at her since she'd first come home and at first glance, Mystic would've given it all to him. He was one of the sexiest men she'd ever laid eyes on. Yet, slowly she changed her mind as started to notice all the *rats* he had coming and going, out of his house.

Mystic looked at Fred and gave him a playful frown and hit him on the shoulder. She looked to Punkin, then to Breeze.

"Umm, I gotta go see my P.O. and drop. I'll be back."

"Aight bitch, what you tellin' me fo'? I ain't yo' damn babysitter. Gone!"

Mystic chuckled as she walked down the steps. Fred asked her if she wanted a ride.

"Naw, I'm good. I'm gon' catch the bus but thanks anywayz."

She walked down the block towards West Florissant until she was out of their eye sight. She cut through a vacant house's yard to the alley. She walked up the alley, back to their house and grabbed her bag from the side of the garage. She headed back down the alley towards the bus stop.

She had only gotten half way to the bus stop before she ran into Lil Curtis, coming towards her across the street. As always, he way dressed in a one of the craziest outfits she had ever seen. He looked like Tyler Perry's, *Mr. Brown.* Dressed in a pair of green, beige and white checkered shorts, along with a checkered blue and yellow t-shirt. He had his tube socks pulled all the way up to his knees and he had on house shoes.

"Aey baby, where you going?"

Mystic put her finger up to her mouth and gestured for him to lower his voice.

"Lil Curtis, I gotta go do somethin' that I don't want *nobody* to know about and if anybody asks, you ain't seen me."

Lil Curtis held up both of his hands in front of him.

"I got you baby, I ain't gon' tell nobody."

Then he walked past her, put his hands up to his mouth and yelled.

"Aey er'body, Mystic sneakin' off."

Mystic threw her hand on her hip.

"Lil Curtis!"

He looked to her playfully.

"Well, I ain't gon' tell nobody else, for a small fee of course. Buy yo' boy a cold one or somethin'."

Mystic chuckled, reached in her pocket and pulled out a twenty dollar bill.

"Here, this should be way more than enough to keep you quiet."

"Fo sho'...aey and if you need me to run away wit' you next time, just holla."

Mystic shook her head.

"I'm good."

Lil Curtis ran his hands down his chest and flicked his tongue out his mouth.

"It's all good, I know you scared of all this."

Mystic chuckled and continued down the street towards the bus stop.

She boarded the Florissant and headed downtown. The bus dropped her off in front of the Greyhound Bus Station on Cass Ave. She had a thirty minute wait and decided to run across the street to the KFC. As she stood in line at KFC, Mystic started to get nervous.

What am I doing? I'm on probation and shit. What if I get caught? Am I really willing to take this kind of chance for him? What if what Man said was right?

She tossed the questions around in her head until she reached the ticket counter of bus station. The point of no return had been reached as she handed the clerk her money.

Mystic began to think of her daughter. She had had so many plans when she came home. That plan was to do whatever it took to get her baby back. But on a Walgreen's salary, she knew she'd never be able to afford a lawyer to battle the military for custody. She hoped in her heart, that if she did this for Spider, he would help her get an attorney and get back her baby girl. So, she exhaled, took a seat, said a prayer and waited for her boarding call.

Chapter Twenty Seven

Tee-Tee had just walked out of JMar's and begun walking up West Florissant towards Park Lane when he spotted her. Cocamo blew his horn to get her attention and pulled the jeep beside her.

"I need to holla at you."

Tee-Tee waved her hand, ignored him and continued walking up Park Lane. Cocamo pulled the jeep over, hopped out and called after her.

"Aey, I know you hear me talkin' to you. I said I need to holla at you."

"Holla at the bitch you was just with," she snapped back at him. "When I wanted to talk to you about something, you were too busy. So what, you got yo' shit off and now you got time to fuck wit' me?"

Cocamo was so tempted to walk away and say fuck it but he knew if he did, he'd never get up the nerve to say to her what he came to say. He had fought with himself over and over again concerning his feelings for her. It was now or never.

Tee-Tee had turned from him and kept walking towards the alley she used to get to Mimika.

"Here you go with all that tryin' to be hard shit. Fo' yo' muthafuckin' information, I put the bitch out cause I couldn't stop thinkin' bout yo' wanna-be-tough ass!"

She stopped dead in her tracks. Her heart had fluttered when he said that and it totally caught her off guard.

Did he just say he couldn't fuck the bitch cause he couldn't stop thinkin' bout me?"

She turned to face him.

"Huh? What you just say?"

"You can huh, you can hear. You heard me, I couldn't stop thinkin' bout you. I had to come make sure you was good. I don't know why; protectin' my investment I guess. But yeah, I had to check on you."

Tee-Tee threw her hand up at him and shook her head. She should've known that was too good to be true. Cocamo caring about something, someone other than money and pussy. She needed a reason from him, any reason not to go through with Big Slug's plan. She didn't want to hurt him. Yes, at first she too was all about the money but the more time she'd spent with him, the more she began to feel for him.

Tee-Tee started walking again down the alley. She just needed more time to figure out what she was gonna do. She had walked and walked since she'd left his porch earlier that evening but she still couldn't figure out her best move. He was not making it any easier. The closer she got to Mimika, Cocamo did something he'd never thought he'd do in his life. He went after her.

He jogged and caught up with her at the end of the alley. He grabbed her arm and turned her to him once again.

"Look, I didn't mean that. I mean, yes you are my investment but not in the way I just said it. Look, I ain't good at all this kinda shit. But I came to see about you, ain't that enough?"

Tee-Tee looked at him. She could honestly feel the sincerity in his words, no matter how un-romantic they were. He liked her too and like her, he didn't know what to do about it.

He looked down the alley towards Park Lane.

"You comin' or what?"

163

It was the best she would get out of him, she told herself. She knew that what he'd said alone, took a lot for him to say. She shook her head and told him yes, she would go home with him. As they walked back to the jeep, Tee-Tee silently wished that all of this could play out differently. She wanted Big Slug and his plan to just disappear but she knew it wasn't going be. She had actually succeeded in what he'd told her to do.

She had manipulated Cocamo into caring about her and herself into caring about him.

Whatever's gonna happen is gonna happen tonight, she told herself as she climbed into the jeep. *Either I'm gon' tell him what Big Slug's fat ass is up to and he's gon' kill me. Else I'm gon' have to fulfill my contract with Slug and I'm gon' have to kill Coco.*

In her eyes, there was no tomorrow, only tonight. She had to make a choice. She just wanted one more night; just a little more time with him before things got out of control.

Chapter Twenty Eight

When the bus pulled in to the Greyhound Station on Illinois Street in Indianapolis, Mystic pulled out her cell phone to call Remo. It was a 3:45 p.m. and Remo was expecting her call. She searched through her phone log and realized she'd used the house phone to call him earlier and she'd left the piece of paper with his name on it, on her bed.

Damn, now I gotta call home.

She dialed the number to the house and Breeze answered the phone.

"Damn, we thought yo' *PO* locked yo' ass up, you been gon' so long. Don't you gotta be at work in fifteen minutes?"

"Naw, I was off," she lied. It was easier that way in case their tried to come up to the store, which they often did, to get free stuff from Mystic.

"And I left my PO about three hours ago. I ran into a friend of mine at the Probation Office that was locked up with me and we been hangin'. Can you do me a favor and go look on my bed and give me that number off that piece of paper that says Remo?"

You could hear her exhale through the receiver. Breeze smacked her lips and headed down the steps.

"Ya *boyfriend* been callin' like crazy. He said he'll call back later cause I thought you had to work, my bad."

"It's cool, what's the number?"

Breeze gave Mystic the number and told her don't be out in the streets all day. Mystic told her she would call if she was, then hung up the phone. She didn't need Breeze asking her too many more questions. Mystic dialed the number to Remo's cell phone and told him she was in town.

The plan was for them to meet up at the station, Mystic get in the car, make the transaction and get back on the next bus which, was leaving in the next two hours.

As simple as it sounded, nothing goes that simple in the game, especially when you're dealing with someone shady, like Remo.

When he arrived, he told Mystic that he'd left the package at the hotel because the police where out in full force when he left the room. Mystic gritted her teeth but remained silent. She understood that she was on somebody else's dime and time. She also knew that nobody wanted a case, if it could be avoided.

So when black Range Rover pulled up to the familiar Holiday Inn East, Mystic thought nothing of it. Even when they entered the room on the second floor and his business partners weren't there, she only felt a small sense of uneasiness; that was about to change.

Remo locked the door behind Mystic and sucked his teeth. He had other plans for Mystic, before sealing the deal. He knew she was in a vulnerable position and he intended to take full advantage of it.

"So, did you bring all the paper?"

Mystic nodded her head.

"Yeah, all of it."

Remo walked over to the drawer, opened it and called Mystic over to view its contents. He wanted her to think that everything would go nice, smooth and according to plan.

Mystic pulled out the crumpled brown paper bag, Perez had given her the night before. She had never taken the time to even count it. She handed the bag to Remo and stood off to the side as he removed the bills from the bag and began to count it.

When he reached the desired amount, gave her back eight, one hundred dollar bills.

"Good thing I'm honest, huh?" he said, blowing her a kiss.

He grabbed the duffel bag from Mystic and began placing the Ceram wrapped squares of weed into her bag. Mystic felt a little better knowing that their time together was soon coming to a close. She was ready to get back to Saint Louis. When Remo zipped up the bag, Mystic let out a silent sigh. She was extended her hand to him to retrieve her goods but Remo didn't hand it to her.

Instead, he tossed it over onto the other full sized bed, opposite the one Mystic was standing next too. She got a queasy feeling in her stomach, something was about to go wrong.

I knew this shit seemed to easy… I shoulda known.

Remo walked over towards the bed.

"So yo' man is locked down, huh? How much time he lookin' at?" Remo asked, fishing for answers from her. He knew that if he went through went his plan and she told Spider what happened; he would have to deal with him some day. Although Remo wasn't too worried about it. No man in the game was stupid enough to bring war to somebody else's territory. And Spider against Remo, was like bringing a knife to a gun fight.

Mystic looked off to the wall.

"I don't know. I need to get this back home and do what I gotta do to get him home. He has a bail hearing in a few days."

"Umm, a few days, huh? I know that nigga going crazy right now. Got a fine bitch like you out here in the streets, on her own. In places she ain't grown enough to be, doin' thangs she wish she ain't have to do. Just to get his punk ass out the joint."

Mystic rolled her eyes. First off, she didn't take to kindly to being called a bitch by his ugly ass and secondly, she really had no understanding of what hell he meant by the things she had to do.

"What things? *This?* It's good. He would do the same for me. So, can we move this along? I can take a cab back to the bus station."

Remo sneered.

"You love that nigga all like that?" he asked her, patting the bed beside him.

Mystic knew exactly where he was going with the bullshit. It was Perez all over again but this time, she didn't have Man to call and come to her rescue. She was on Remo's battle ground and from the way it seemed, would have to play by Remo's rules.

Mystic walked over to the bed and hesitantly eased down beside him. She didn't look at him; she just stared down at the floor. He grossed her out from the first moment she'd ever laid eyes on him. The pits in his face, the crooked teeth and the smell of his breath. Now here he was, taking advantage of a bad situation and making it worse.

He kissed her on her shoulder. Mystic cringed at the feel of his crusted and cracked lips. He continued to move up to her neck.

"I really gotta to go," Mystic said.

Remo reached into the waist line of his jeans and pulled out his pistol. A shiny, glock .45 caliber pistol. He placed it on the night stand beside him as if to say to Mystic, *you'll leave, when I say you'll leave.*"

"I know you don't wanna leave here without what you came here fo', right?" he asked her as he continued to kiss her on her cheek. He tried to force her to turn her face towards him but Mystic yanked it away. He was so disgusting to her.

Remo chuckled at her move. He placed his hand underneath her t-shirt and grabbed her breast. The only way Mystic could describe what she was feeling, was as if someone was rubbing a slab of concrete against her flesh. His face felt rocky and his hands were rough and nasty.

This shit is so fuckin' disgustin'! She thought to herself.

She never broke her focus on the floor. Mystic twiddled her thumbs together tightly as he un-snapped her bra in the back.

There were a million thoughts running through her mind at the time. Why was she there? Why had she really made the trip to Indy? Why was she risking her freedom and losing her daughter? Why? Her answer was simple… she loved him. With every fiber in her body, she loved him. Married or not, she loved him.

He had broken down walls around her; she hadn't even known she'd built. He'd made her body respond to sex in ways she never dreamed imaginable. Yes, she loved him and she also knew, at that moment, she'd take this hell and turn it into heaven, once her man came home.

Remo had removed all her clothes by now and Mystic lay back on the multi-colored, floral spread, with her legs slightly apart. It felt as if a wet dog was licking her clit, as she felt his slob run down to her butt crack. It was gross. He put his hands underneath her butt, trying to force her to grind with his face but she couldn't even pretend she was enjoying it.

He towered above her, jacking off his child-like penis, in an attempt to make it hard. He took his knee and pushed her legs to the side once he finally had an erection. Mystic glanced up at what looked to be drool coming from his mouth.

"Yeah, I'm finna tear this pussy up!" he smirked.

Mystic quickly moved her head to the side as he lowered his body down, close to hers. He began searching for the opening to her mommy, with his hand. Mystic shifted her eyes to the bag of weed beside her.

It'll all be worth it when it's him who's inside me.

It had never even occurred to her that he'd found the way inside her, until she heard him breathing. She couldn't feel a thing. He, however, was chanting and panting as if he were a Mandingo warrior.

"Spider ain't hittin' it like this, is he baby?"

He didn't even wait for a response, not to mention, Mystic wasn't about to give him one, before he continued.

"Ohhhh, this pussy is so good. You like dat? You like the way this dick feels?"

Mystic blinked from the sweat, dripping from his forehead, onto her face.

You gotta be shittin' me! No this nigga ain't sweatin' like he really doin' somethin'!"

"Ahhhhhhh shit! I'm finna fill you up baby! Can I cum? Can I cum? Can…?"

Hell naw!

Mystic pushed him off of her, as he began to spasm and shoot juices all over his stomach. He let out the grossest sound she'd ever heard. He sounded like a wounded hound dog. There was no way she was going to risk getting' pregnant by his ugly ass.

He flopped down next to her so exhausted, like he'd just run the Boston Marathon. Mystic quickly got up off the bed and ran into the bathroom. She turned the shower to its hottest level.

I gotta wash all of this nigga off me, now!

She walked back into the room to grab all of her clothes. Remo was now sitting up and watching TV. As Mystic headed back to the bathroom, she felt something loud and hard, hit the back of her left leg; so hard, it almost tripped her. Remo had thrown the duffel bag at her.

"Pleasure doin' business wit' you, Ma."

Mystic picked up the bag and decided she didn't even want to hang around long enough to shower. She just wanted to get the fuck away from him. She dropped the bag; stood right there, in the bathroom doorway, dressed grabbed her shit and headed out the door.

She didn't speak a word; she just wanted to get going. Get far away from him as possible. Mystic got the elevator and headed down for the lobby. She asked the clerk to call her a cab and stood outside until it pulled up.

When she got inside, she slowly unzipped the bag and glanced down at its contents. It seemed to all be there; not that she would know if it wasn't. She lay her head back against the seat and stared out the window as the cab took her back to Illinois Street. She was almost there. She had made it this far and she hoped all would go well on her way back home. She prayed so hard that Spider was worth all the drama and all the trouble.

She took out her cell phone and placed a call to Man. He didn't answer but she left him a message to meet her at the bus station at 11pm. She told him that she'd explain everything to him then and begged him not to say anything to anyone. She needed his help. Mystic, knowing Man the way she did, knew that that was all she needed to say; he'd be there.

Chapter Twenty Nine

"...there comes a time, when love can fade away and it came across for you and I. Now I don't know how or where to go from here. I really don't know just what to do, so baby can you tell me. Where do we go from here? Do we walk away or do we keep on tryin'..."

  The music calmed her soul, as the jeep came to a halt in the driveway of Cocamo's house. He exited the jeep, followed by Tee-Tee and walked up onto the porch. He waved at his neighbors Punkin, and Breeze, sitting on the porch. He search for Mystic but she wasn't there.

  "You know yo' peeps got caught up, right?" Punkin asked him, puffing on a blunt.

  "Yeah, I heard. I see you still smokin' though."

  "Yeah, but it's some bullshit from round da corner."

Cocamo looked to Punkin and smiled

  "Give me a minute. I got somethin' fo' you."

  Cocamo opened the door and let Tee-Tee inside. She didn't wait for an invitation to sit down. She placed her purse down onto the coffee table and turned to him.

  "You want a drink?"

Cocamo raised his eyebrow.

  "You gon' fix me a drink? In *my* house? Damn, you doin' it like that?"

  "Nigga you want a drink or not?"

"Do yo' thang," he told her. "You know where everythang at," he said, going into his room to retrieve Punkin a sack from his own personal stash. He walked next door onto the porch and handed it to her.

He turned to Breeze and and asked her where Mystic was. Breeze replied that she didn't know.

He hit Breeze on the leg and walked back over to his house.

Breeze turned to Punkin and laughed.

"Damn, Mystic got all these nigga's after her."

"Shit, she got her head so far stuck up Spider's ass that she don't see that that nigga right there is the best one out of them all," Punkin said, referring to Cocamo.

When Cocamo entered the house, Tee-Tee was over at the radio. She turned the station to *100.3 The Beat* and turned up the volume. Cocamo chuckled and shook his head. He liked it...the way she was taking control of things. She moved around the house as if she was a permanent fixture. He found that cute.

The music had Tee-Tee gyrating in the kitchen as she fixed him a glass of Patron, straight up. She danced her way over to the cabinet and grabbed another glass. She poured herself a drink and took a swallow, then another. No matter what the night brought, she couldn't face it with a sober mind. Sober, there was no way she could ever hurt him. She'd have to be damn near plastered.

"... girl you got a big ol' ass and bow legs; a lot of head and all the shit that I want, sexy muthafucka. You actin' like you want it right now; let a nigga know, is we gon' fuck tonight. My dick is getting' rock hard, oh my god; it's gonna be some fuckin' tonight. Take them panties off or pull them things off to the side and let a nigga know; is we gon' fuck tonight..."

Cocamo stood in the doorway of the kitchen and smiled as Tee-Tee moved to the beat. He like the way she rolled her hips like Beyonce. It drove him crazy and made him hard. He walked over behind her and grabbed her around her waist.

"You hungry?"

"You cookin'?"

"I do a lil' somethin'," he told her, hitting her on the ass. "Gon' get comfortable. I got you."

Tee-Tee handed him his drink, grabbed her drink and headed for the living room. She turned off the radio and turned on the TV. She leaned up to the table and rolled up a blunt. She grabbed the Garcia Vega off the table, split it with her fingernail and filled it with her favorite *cush*. She ran her tongue across the paper, twirled it around in her mouth and grabbed her lighter.

She took a puff of the blunt as she watched some white man stroke the hell out of Halle Berry in *Monster's Ball*. Her thoughts drifted to Cocamo, in the kitchen, cooking her something to eat. Things like that were just un-heard of with him. He never allowed a female, any female to get that comfortable.

Tee-Tee was simply testing him when she came in earlier and just started touching things uninvited, to see if he had meant all those things he had said to her earlier, when he'd found her. It was touching her, that he did.

The aroma from the kitchen smelled so nice.

I can't believe this nigga is making me dinner! What am I gon' do? Everything feels so right; right now anyway. If I don't go through with this, Slug could wind up taking me out. If I do, I'll hurt the only man I've come to have feelings for. Is the 'hood credibility really worth all this? God, please help me figure this out.

Tee-Tee sat on the couch, pondering back and forth until Cocamo leaned down and handed her a plate with bite sized pieces of T-bone steak, smothered potatoes, eggs and toast.

Her eyes bucked open when she saw the spread he'd prepared special, just for her. Her heart completely melted when he placed a paper towel across her lap. Cocamo handed her the silverware and placed the ketchup and hot sauce on the table.

His thoughtfulness almost made her cry but the 'hood in her wouldn't allow her too. She couldn't afford to show emotions in front of him. She may have to stand in front of him with a gun pointed at him later that night. How could she expect him to take her seriously if she sat there and cried over something as simple as dinner?

He went back into the kitchen and Tee-Tee shook her head.

Damn! Why he wait so long to show some type of interest. I been knowing this nigga fo' hella. We could've been on top of the game together, year's ago. Now look at us; he's interested and living to see my next meal depends on me taking him out.

Cocamo came back into the living room with his food in hand. He sat down on the couch beside her.

"Everything aight?"

Tee-Tee couldn't help but smile.

"It's da bomb. It's really is… where did you learn to cook like this."

"My grandma taught me. She always told me that one day I might fall in love with a woman who can burn bricks, so I needed to learn to take care of myself."

They enjoyed the late night meal side-by-side, watching the movie. They took turns, staring at each other while the other one wasn't looking. Their pride was being tested and laid out on the line for either one of them to step on the others'. Both wondering how they'd let their guard down with one another. How they'd gotten in the position they were in and what they were going to do about it.

Cocamo cleared the dishes when they were finished and Tee-Tee volunteered to wash them. As she stood at the sink, rinsing the dishes, Cocamo came up behind her. Her standing there, washing his dishes, turned him on something terrible. He pressed his hardness against her lower back.

He reached around her and gripped her breasts. He squeezed firmly as he whispered in her ear.

"I don't know what the fuck you doin' to me but I think I'm fuckin' startin' to like it."

Tee-Tee let her head fall back and exhaled.

"I'm glad cause I think I'm startin' to like doin' it to you."

Cocamo slid his hands down her stomach and unbuttoned her jeans. He un-zipped her zipper and slowly began pulling down her pants. He pushed his fingers inside her from behind. Tee-Tee moaned and gripped the dish towel in her hands.

"Keep washing the dishes," he whispered. "Don't stop, you hear me? Don't fuckin' move."

He used his free hand to unbutton his jeans. He pulled out his jimmy and began sliding it across her ass cheeks. When her mommy was soak and wet, he guided the tip of his jimmy inside her. He normally would've tried to tear her back out the frame but tonight; tonight, he just wanted to enjoy her and savor her.

177

He didn't rush; he took his own sweet time. Stroking her long and deep. Tee-Tee took her hands from the water and held onto the ledge of the sink. He felt so good to her. She hiked herself up on her tippy-toes to allow him access to go deeper. She grinded against him and she dwelled in satisfaction as he moaned out in pleasure.

This night was different. They felt each other, they connected to each other and they embraced the feelings they had come to have for each other.

Cocamo held onto the ledge of the sink, fingers interlocked with hers and bent his knees. He could completely lift her off the ground. Tee-Tee could damn near feel him in her chest. Her body was in heaven as Cocamo brought her to her peak three times before cumming himself inside her.

He let his juices flow and laid his head on the back of hers. They both were breathing so hard and sweat was dripping down from his head to hers.

"Let's go to bed."

Tee-Tee couldn't have heard him right. Even he second guessed the words he had just let come from his mouth.

Did he just ask me to spend the night with him?

He placed his foot in between her ankles and down onto her jeans. He told her to step out of her pants. He bent down and picked them up, grabbed her by the hand and led her to the bedroom.

Chapter Thirty

When Mystic exited the bus station, the black jeep was waiting right out front for her. Man exited the jeep, walked around to the passenger side, opened the door for her and took the bag from her. He threw it into the back seat, walked around the jeep and got in. Once inside, he simply sat back and looked at her. He was waiting on her to explain what the hell she was doing at the bus station.

"So what's this about, Mimi?" he asked her, putting the jeep in gear.

"Okay, promise you won't start yelling and shit Man. I went to Indy with the money I got from Perez and…" she began.

"You did what?" he interrupted.

Mystic turned to face him.

"I said promise. Look Man, I know you said these streets ain't fo' me but you're wrong." She said, reaching to the back seat and grabbing the bag.

She unzipped it and put it on his lap.

"Whatever it is I need to be in me, is in me, especially when it comes to someone I love."

Man looked through the bag and then back to her.

"Zip this shit up! I ain't impressed, Mimi," he said, throwing the bag back onto her lap.

"What the fuck is wrong with you? This nigga got a gold tip on his dick or somethin'? Cause I swear, you are doin' some of the dumbest shit I've ever seen in my life, to win this nigga."

Mystic took offense to that statement. Was not he the one who was using her very own sister to go out of town and pick up his dope for him?

"And how is this any different than what Breeze does for you?"

"What you mean? What Breeze do fo' me, *profits* Breeze. I take damn good care of mine. What assurance do you have that this married muthafuckin' nigga is gon' take care of you? You fun to him right now, don't you get that. Cause I promise you, when that bitch find out he fuckin' you, it's a done deal! He want you cause he know all the other nigga's in the hood want you. It's a ego thang, Mimi. You ain't got no business risking yo' freedom or yo' life fo' that matter, over a nigga who lay next to another bitch every muthafuckin' night. No matter what he tell you, all that lil' sweet shit he whisper in yo' ear while he fuckin' you, he gon' always, always go home baby," he told, his voice quieting down.

"I've seen it to many times," he continued. "My female patna's, my family... hell, even my own momma. She wasted her whole muthafuckin' life following up behind a nigga that was married and the muthafucka drove her to her grave with bullshit promises.

You got potential Mimi, potential to be anything you wanna be. The rest of them around you ain't gon' be nothin' but what they are. But you... you got a chance to do somethin' different, be somethin' special and I for one, don't want to see you fuck that up. Not over a nigga I know ain't right fo' you."

Mystic sat quietly as he spoke. While it was nice to know Man thought of her in that way, she still undoubtedly believed that Spider would be with her if she did this for him.

"Man, can you help me or not?"

Man just shook his head.

"Damn, is it that serious?"

She paused.

"For me, yes."

Man exhaled.

"For your sake Mimi, I hope it's that serious for him, too. Leave it with me, I got you."

He drove her to the highway and hit 70 West towards the house.

"Wait! You can't drop me off; they think I've been with a girlfriend all day."

Man snickered.

"I got you."

He pulled in front of his cousin Kamira's house on Ruskin and put the car in park.

"I'll be right back."

He returned followed by the young woman. She looked straight out of *ghetto* magazine. Her hair was a variety of colors, her lip pierced with a big hoop in the middle and her outfit was straight out of *skank* fashions.

"This my peeps, Kamira. She's gon' take you home for me."

Mystic got out of the jeep and gave Man a hug.

"Thanks Man. I know you think I'm trippin' but I'll be fine, I promise."

Man nodded his head, got in his jeep and took off.

Mystic jumped in the tan, beat up Maxima with Kamira and put on her seat belt. As soon as she turned the ignition, out blasted **Keisha Cole's**, *Let It Go*.

"Oohhh girl, that's my jam!"

Mystic hunched her eyes brows and looked out the window.

Go figure!

As they rode up to Riverview Boulevard, the words sort of hit Mystic unexpectedly.

"... I understand why you wanna try, make him stay home late at night, but wanna go, he'll be gon' no lie. I can't explain how many times I tried, how many times I cried, thinkin' about mine and where he might be..."

Mystic sat back thinking as the car turned onto Harney.

Am I turning into one of those women that I despised for sleepin' with my husband?

She paused.

Oh well, they didn't give a fuck, so why should I?

She waited as the car rolled up the block and Keisha Cole continued to lay it down.

"...but now I get if he don't wanna, love you the right way, he ain't gonna. It ain't where he's at, it's where he, where he wanna be. If he ain't love you, the way he, then let it go...."

Punkin and Breeze was sitting on the porch when the Maxima pulled up in front of the house. Mystic thanked the girl and closed the car door. When she reached the porch, no one asked any questions and Mystic was glad for that. She simply went inside and headed straight for the shower.

As she lay in the bed, thoughts of Spider, Remo and Man, swirled around her head. She felt a tear roll down the side of her face. She wanted this to be everything she was hoping it could be between her and Spider.

Although she had walked into the situation blind at first, once she found out he was married, she *chose* to stay. That meant she chose all the consequences and bullshit that came along with it. She was okay with that. She just didn't want to come up short in *all* areas of the deal.

It would be the next evening when Man hit her phone and told her, he had something for her. She had just finished talking to Spider on the phone and she had told him that she'd be at his bail hearing with bells on. But it was then, that she had gotten her first dose of harsh reality. Spider had told her that her coming to his bail hearing wouldn't be a good idea because his wife would be there. Mystic stared down in disbelief at the receiver.

I know he ain't just say that? His wife? The same bitch that just said she was gon' leave him in there?

Suddenly Man's words hit her like a ton of bricks.

"They always go home, Mimi. Wifey is always first."

Spider asked her to try and understand. He needed her to sign out his bond. He told Mystic to give the money to Perez and have him take it to his wife. Mystic, frustrated by then, agreed just to get off the phone.

"I'll be there to see you as soon as I touch down, Mommy."

Mystic hung up the phone and felt the tears roll down her face. He had no idea what she had gone through to get him out and he had literally pushed her out of the satisfaction of seeing him walk out jail. Being the first one he wrapped his arms around.

Everyone in the game has a place.

That lesson, she had just learned first hand. She told Man to come on through. When he arrived, he found her sitting on the bed, wiping her face. Breeze was right behind him.

"What's wrong with you?" Breeze asked her.

"I was just thinking about my baby," she lied.

"Who, Spider?"

"Naw, Tia."

Man sat down beside her and hugged her, which made Breeze kinda jealous. She was tired of people always portraying Mystic as a little helpless baby. So what she'd been to jail. In Breeze's eyes, she was dumb for staying with her ex-husband for as long as she did and having absolutely nothing to show for it. She turned and walked out the room, which to Mystic, was a good thing.

"You sure that's what's wrong?" he asked her.

Mystic nodded her head. She couldn't dare tell Man what Spider had told her. It would let him know he was right and Mystic didn't want to face that.

He handed her four, rubber band stacks of money and told her to put it up.

"I only did this shit fo' you, you know that."

Mystic smiled and leaned her head on his shoulder.

"Thanks again, Man."

"Let me go get this damn girl. You know she hate it when I pay anybody some attention other than her."

Mystic chuckled.

When he left the room, she looked at the money. She had to figure out a way to get the money to Spider's wife without involving Perez. She went upstairs and walked out onto the porch with the money, tucked deep in her pocket. Punkin was sitting on the front, talking to Unc. Mystic had found her way. She knew Unc would deliver it for her if she explained to him what was going on.

"Unc, Spider asked me to talk to you about something."

Unc followed her in the house, back to the kitchen. Mystic handed him the money and told him what she needed him to do. He said he'd take care of it without hesitation. Now all she had to do was wait. In less than twelve hours, she'd have her man back in her arms or so she thought.

Chapter Thirty One

Tee-Tee was becoming overwhelmed. Cocamo was making her feel thing's she had never felt before. All of it, the entire evening was so out of character for him. He may not have been able to say what he felt for her but in his own way, he was letting her know that he was digging her.

He laid her down on the bed, pulled the covers halfway over her body, turned out the light and lay down beside her. No words needed to be spoken between them, it wasn't necessary. Tee-Tee's mind was in a million places. Her thoughts were volleying back and forth between what to do about Big Slug and how Cocamo was making her feel inside.

She couldn't settle down her mind and she had good reason. The night was slipping away and something had to come to an end. No matter how good he made her feel... no matter how much she enjoyed being there in his arms... she had to end a life... his or hers.

Cocamo reached over to his night stand and picked up his mini blunt from the ashtray. He lit up his weed, took a few puffs and handed it to Tee-Tee.

"Now I gotta find me another medicine man with that good cause this dumb ass nigga done got caught up, doin' stupid shit."

Tee-Tee shook her head in agreement.

"Maybe Perez 'nem will hold it down fo' him."

"Shit, them bitch ass nigga's probably told on him in the first fuckin' place," he said, choking from the smoke.

"I don't fuck wit' none of these simp ass nigga's round here. Nigga's is worst than some of these bitches out here. Nigga's hearts pump envy and greed too. They'll either cross you to get what you got or move up to yo' spot. That's why I roll solo. The last muthafuckin' thing I'ma do is snitch on my damn self."

Cocamo went on and on until he no longer received a response from Tee-Tee. He looked down and saw her sleeping soundly on his chest. He let her be, He simply reached over and put out the roach in the ashtray and stared up at the ceiling.

He kicked back, turned on the 42 inch flat screen TV but muted the sound. He turned the stereo to Foxy 95.5 FM and listened as Lonnie from *Lonnie's Love Lounge* played a song that for the moment eased the doubt in his mind concerning the feelings in his heart that were building for Tee-Tee.

"...come here, let's talk dear. There are things inside me, I want you to hear. I wanna soak into you like rain. Make love until my energy drains. And as lust erases all shame; you'll scream my name out of pleasure not pain. If you'll just say yes, I'll do the rest..."

Cocamo lay back and thought to himself. He often wondered why he had such a deep distrust of women. He knew that somehow if had to do with the fact that his mother was never there for him.

Raised by his grandmother; she tried really hard to keep him from the streets but Cocamo was drawn to the life of money, power and respect that the streets brought him. He lived his life as if the world revolved around him and keep everyone, especially women at a distance.

Now he lay in bed, next to a woman, his gut feelings told him not to trust; yet his heart was telling his to let go and give it a try. The more he tried to fight it, the more he found her getting a little closer to breaking through his walls.

He leaned down a placed a soft kiss on her forehead. He looked over to the light glowing from inside her purse. The vibration growing more and more irritating by the second. Cocamo couldn't help but to wonder who it was, blowing her up that time a night. He had a pretty good idea... Big Slug.

He had made it up in his mind that in the morning, he would tell she had to quit working for Big Slug because they in competition for money and customers. Her working for him would only bring problems between him and her or him and Slug. Either way, it would be drama that he didn't have time for in his life.

The vibration continued and his curiosity got the best of him. When she turned her body from his chest, he saw his opportunity and he took it.

He stood up. Walked over to the dresser and picked up the phone from inside her purse. When he flipped it open, sure enough it was Big Slug blowing her up. She had like twelve missed calls from him.

Damn, is she fuckin' this nigga? I know damn well he ain't blowin' her up over them petty ass rocks she sellin' fo' him.

The phone began to vibrate again, in his hand. He glanced back to find Tee-Tee still sleeping soundly. Cocamo hit the *send* button and brought the phone up to his ear.

"...Aey, you betta have a good muthafuckin' reason for not answerin' my call, bitch. Betta yet, I'm gon' assume you over there handlin' business with that pussy ass nigga Coco. That nigga betta be dead already or else..."

Cocamo snapped the phone close and hung up on him. His initial thought was to go at him on the phone and tell him to meet him in the streets. But Cocamo moved smarter than that. He always tried making sure he had the upper hand in any situation he found himself in. This one was definitely one that he needed to get control of and quick. From what he'd just heard, the woman he'd bailed out of jail and opened up his heart to, was sent to take away his life.

> *So it's a game; a game to get me out the way, huh? I gave this bitch my money? My time? I got this funky hoe outta jail and fo' what? You think you can take my life? Well, let the games begin.*

It would've been easy to simply just kill her while she was lying there sleep but he needed a way to make the entire situation to his advantage, not just part of it. To kill her, wouldn't rid him of the threat of Big Slug trying to finish the job he'd sent her to do.

He needed to think. He walked into the living room with Tee-Tee's phone still in his hand. He sat down on the couch and plotted his next move. Every step had to calculated. One wrong step to the left or to the right and it would cost him his life for sure.

Chapter Thirty Two

Mystic spent most of the night tossing and turning. She was very hurt over what Spider had said to her but she was also anxious to see him. She missed him terribly and couldn't wait to lay eyes on him, no matter how upset she was.

She got out of the bed, glanced over at the clock on the nightstand and smiled.

"Won't be much longer," she said.

Spider's bail hearing was in less than an hour.

"I gotta get it together."

Mystic walked upstairs to the bathroom. While sitting on the toilet, she heard the moaning and rumbling sounds of morning sex, coming from Punkin's room, through the walls. The male voice sounded so familiar. The more he talked, the more Mystic knew she was right about who she thought it was.

Unc? So, he is hittin' Punkin! You go girl! Get that old dick!

She chuckled to herself. She reached over and turned on the shower. She washed up, washed her hair and wrapped herself up in a towel. When she opened the bathroom door, she ran right smack into Unc, creeping out of Punkin's room. It was as if he'd seen a ghost. He looked so embarrassed.

"Oh... uhhh... I thought you'd gon' back downstairs, Niecy."

Mystic giggled and put her hand on his arm.

"It's okay, Unc. I think it's cute... I mean, the you and Punkin thing," she said, continuing to giggle as she walked down the steps to her room.

She knocked on Breeze's door to share her juicy gossip but when she heard Man's voice answer instead, she decided to wait.

"Yeah?"

"Never mind, I'll come back."

"You good?" he asked.

"Yeah."

Mystic went into her room and rolled her eyes.

Damn, er'body gettin' broke off but me! It's good though, mine's will be here soon, she told herself, looking at the clock again.

Mystic dried her hair, flat ironed it and wrapped it up. She arched her eyebrows, did her nails and her feet in a soft pink color. She picked out Spider's favorite floral, pink sundress to wear.

Time was moving along and Mystic's heart was leaping with joy. By noon, she was dressed, hair flowing down, smelling good and beautiful. She went upstairs and out the front door. She sat down on the porch, planning to sit there until she saw the Suburban hit the corner.

After another hour or so, Punkin and Unc joined her on the porch.

"Damn, you makin' sure that nigga see you today, huh?" Unc said.

"I feel you girl," Punkin chimed in. "Let that nigga know what he been missin'. Sometimes they need a lil' remindin' to stop sleepin' on what's right in front of they faces."

Unc looked over to Punkin and shook his head.

"That's my queue."

He walked next door and Mystic waited until he was inside, then she turned to Punkin.

"Ummm, when did this happen?" she asked, pointing between the two houses.

"It's been brewin' for like forever girl. I'd go over there to watch the stories and smoke with him. He might *accidentally* rub against my titty or somethin' and I might *accidentally* rub against that dick, you hear me? Shit, big bitches need love to and fuck that... Unc fine as a muthafucka, shit, so why not? It would've been gone down but he was so worried about ruinin' our friendship but I was like, fuck a friendship! Last night he was so high, he couldn't do nothin' but fall asleep in my bed durin' the movie. This mornin' he woke up with his dick in my mouth...*how u doin'?*"

"Sooo... how was it? Cause from the bathroom, it sounded like it was da bomb!"

Punkin inhaled her blunt.

"Shit, bitch... you ever seen that KY commercial, with the couple sittin' in the bed, talkin' 'bout how they tried the intense lubricating gel and the bitch fell off the cliff when she bust one? Picture the gel, coupled with a nigga that's packing nine inches of raw dick! Now, answer that one fo' yo'self."

Mystic laughed.

"Shit, I can imagine."

"I bet you can. If you can't, you bout to find out. That nigga ain't had no pussy in a week. Been up in there with all them hard legs... he ready to hurt somethin'!" Punkin said, handing the blunt to Breeze who had just stepped onto the porch, followed by Man.

He looked to Mystic and held her stare for a minute. She looked down at the ground. She knew he was still upset with her but she was so thankful he decided to help her anyway.

Man wasn't amazed at how beautiful she looked sitting there. To him, she always was. It re-iterated everything he thought about her and Spider's relationship. She was too good for him. He didn't deserve her. He didn't want her near him but he held his piece. The fact was, he kind of admired her for going all out for her man, even if he didn't deserve it. As long as she was safe, he'd let her make her own choices and decisions... along with her own mistakes.

One by one, the porch filled with the usual gang and Mystic was glad to see Toi, Hank, Harvey and DC. Yet, the one face she was dying to see; hadn't arrived.

It wasn't until Lil' Curtis came walking through the gangway of the houses next door, that Mystic had finally heard any news. When Toi asked Lil' Curtis where he'd been, Lil Curtis pointed towards the corner.

"I been round 'there tryin' to get a celebratory blunt or somethin' from that nigga, Spider."

"He home?" Punkin asked.

"Yeah, that ashy ass nigga home, walkin' like his ass is tight from squeezin' it together in there all week. I told 'em his shit

193

done bagged all the way up to his throat cause I smell it on his breath," he chuckled, along with everyone else.

"He round there 'bout to barbeque."

Mystic's mouth dropped. Man instantly turned to look at her and spit on the ground beside him. He just walked off the front and got in his jeep. He didn't say a word, he just drove off.

Mystic couldn't believe he didn't even call her. Her feelings were so hurt and the more Lil' Curtis talked, the more she was getting pissed off.

Barbeque? How the fuck he gon' do me like that?

She felt her eyes beginning to well up with tears so, she excused herself and went inside the house.

By eight o'clock, the porch eventually cleared one-by-one and Mystic had checked her cell phone for the hundredth time, finally she realized... he wasn't coming.

"Girl, you shouldn't have really expected him to come on his first day back to the crib. He gotta play the good husband role for a while. Make up for all the bullshit he's caused over the last couple weeks. Muthafucka's kickin' in her shit and embarrassing her. He gotta make up fo' that. Yeah, I know I told you, they don't give a fuck 'bout them bitches at home and they don't.

But they do care about they safety net, no matter who it comes from. The place where they can lay they head, no matter what they do or how they do it. As long as they takin' care of that place, they good... they can then do whatever the fuck they want to do. He gotta put that work back in and she probably on his head about 'er little thang right now."

Mystic bit down on the inside of her jaw and shook her head. She wished somebody would have told her all this before she went through all the bullshit she had gone through to get him home to somebody else.

If he was gon' be worried about takin' care of her, hell she should've taken her fat ass to get him out! She should've had to fuck Remo, not me!

She got up off the chair, went inside and headed down stairs. She just wanted the day to be over. She wrapped her hair, pulled off her clothes, turned on the radio, pulled back the covers and cried.

Chapter Thirty Three

As Cocamo sat on the couch, Tee-Tee's phone continued to vibrate. Instincts told him that if Big Slug was on this type of shit, he was near by. He got up off the couch and looked out the window. Sure enough, he spotted the Escalade parked on Harney, facing Mimika with his lights turned off.

Cocamo decided it was time to make his move. He walked back into his bedroom. Tee-Tee was still sleeping like a ton of bricks. He walked over to the bed and retrieved his nine millimeter from underneath his mattress first, then went back over to Tee-Tee's purse and removed her pistol from inside and placed down in the back of his waist.

Her phone began to wiggle again inside his hand. Cocamo flipped open the phone and listened angrily as Big Slug continued to question her about the job he sent her to do. Big Slug kept ranting, raving and threatening to do bodily harm to her if he didn't hear sirens in the air soon.

Somehow, Cocamo didn't hear the threats Big Slug was making against Tee-Tee's life, which may have cleared up some things for him. All he heard was she sent to do him harm and that, he wouldn't stand for.

When Big Slug stopped to take a breath, he didn't hear a response again on the other end of the line and began shouting her name. Cocamo sat down gently on the bed, cocked his gun and held the phone to Tee-Tee's ear. He watched as her eyes popped open at the sound of Big Slug's voice.

Tee-Tee jumped and sat up on the bed. Cocamo closed the phone and Tee-Tee's heart began to beat uncontrollably. Her eyes shifted to the gun in his hand. She knew he knew. She was frozen, she couldn't move a muscle.

196

Cocamo shook his head. He was so upset and everything in him wanted to blow her head off, right then and there but he just stared at her. Waiting for her to try to explain herself but nothing came out.

For Tee-Tee, there was no point in trying to lie to him, she figured she might as well just tell him the truth.

Maybe if I just tell him everything, he'll understand. Maybe even save me from Big Slug.

"So this is it? This is what this was all about? It would be so easy fo' me to kill you right now but you useless to me dead. Yo' bitch ass boss is across the street and he act like he got somethin' to prove. So, what we gon' is we gon' go outside and see just how muthafuckin' big his balls are."

Tee-Tee looked over to her purse on the dresser. Cocamo chuckled.

"That's a done deal," he said turning around to show her, her pistol in the back of his waist.

Tee-Tee could do nothing but drop her head. He pointed for her to exit out his bedroom but Tee-Tee couldn't move from the bedside. She knew that getting up off that bed meant her death, either at Cocamo's hands or Big Slug's hands.

She sat there and wondered what was it all for; what was it all about. She had put the game before every aspect of her life and now here she was, in love for the first time and possibly about to lose her life at his hands. She had played him to get next to him; how could she be upset at the way he handled it once he found out.

Tee-Tee took a deep breath and accepted that things went this way in game. You shoot craps with yo' life when you step in this arena. She always prided herself on being able to hang with the big boys, to be able to hustle and grind at their level. That meant she had to suffer the consequences at that same level.

She stood up and slowly walked towards him. Her eyes searched his face for some sign of compassion. She found none; not one hint of sympathy. Tee-Tee understood his right to be furious but somehow she had hoped he would be a little more lenient after the night they had just shared together.

Cocamo couldn't stand the sight of her at the moment. How could she do him that way? He was more upset with himself than her. He had let his guard down; went against everything his gut had told him about her. He wanted to hurt her something awful. He wanted her to feel the betrayal he was feeling at that moment. Nothing in his heart told him to give her a chance to explain.

"Don't act scared now. *You* fucked up. *You* did this shit. *You* came at me with this bullshit. And yeah, I slipped but you bets believe, fallin' ain't in my genetic make up. So let's go face this muthafuckin' music," he said, pushing Tee-Tee on her shoulder as she passed him on her way out of his bedroom.

Tee-Tee stumbled when he pushed her and caught her balance on the dining room table. It was only then that she knew two things without a doubt. One was the extent of his anger and two was that fact that he really had come to care about her.

She felt her eyes welling up with tears and all the 'hood toughness in the world couldn't keep them from falling. She turned to him and put her hands up.

"It ain't what you think. Please just let me explain. You can't send me out there."

"Oh really? You wanna explain now. Naw, you had plenty of opportunities to holla at me but you didn't. You continued to play this game. One thing 'bout the game, any game but especially *this* game… you gotta be able to finish and finish strong. Check mate bitch, let's go."

Chapter Thirty Four

When the knock finally came from Spider at the front door, it was 72 hours later, early in the morning and Mystic was livid. One side of her, wanted no parts of him; couldn't care less what he had to say but the other side, the other side had missed him terribly. She was confused and she was pissed, severely pissed.

Punkin let him in the house and was the first one to blast him as soon as he entered the front door.

"Damn, nigga! I know that bitch ain't got you helmed up that tough that you couldn't bring yo' ass around the corner, to even say what's up to a bitch? What the fuck? You got my sista sittin' here, stressed the fuck out, waitin' on yo' ass to come see her and here you are, three muthafuckin' days later? I understand you gotta play house and shit, but damn... I know yo' drunk ass done went to the store or somethin' and could've swung by."

"Damn, hi to you too, Punkin."

"Fuck hi! Where's my damn money fo' all them muthafuckin' collect calls?"

He reached in his pocket and peeled off eight, twenty dollar bills and handed them to her.

"Let me know if they more than that. I appreciate you lettin' me call. Now, where's my baby."

"Shit, I don't know about that baby shit, but Mystic downstairs."

Spider snickered at Punkin's remark and headed down the basement steps. He knew Mystic would be a little upset with him but once he explained how things were, he knew she would forgive him. The diamond earrings in his pocket, re-assured him of that. Spider knew she longed for the finer things in life and he wanted to be the one to give them to her. He just couldn't leave his wife to do it.

Mystic had heard the conversation between Punkin and Spider from the bottom of the basement steps. When she heard him coming, she ran into her room, quietly closed the door and lay out across the bed. When he knocked on the door, she turned to face the wall, leaving her back towards the door. When she didn't answer his knock, Spider turned the knob and entered the room.

"Hey Mommy," he said, sitting down beside her on the bed, touching her on her calf.

She didn't respond. She wanted him to know that she was pissed at what he'd done, especially after everything she'd gone through. Although his touch felt so good to her, she had to stand her ground and let him know that he was wrong and she wouldn't tolerate it.

"Sit up baby, let me talk to you."

Mystic still didn't move. Spider kicked his shoes off and lay down beside her, his hardness pressing up against her ass. He rubbed her arm and whispered in her ear.

"I'm so sorry, Mommy. Things have been so fucked up at home. She been on my head at every turn. Pissed off at the raid and just been threatening to do dumb shit like, take my kids from me and shit."

That remark got Mystic to look up at him. She knew all to well how it felt to lose your children. But that fact alone, wouldn't make it all better.

"Okay, I'm understanding that," she said rolling over to face him.

"That's all fine and dandy but what does that have to do with you at least calling?"

She sat up in the bed.

"I sat here all that day, hair combed, wearin' yo' favorite outfit and shit, Waiting to see you pull around the corner. Lookin' like a fool to everybody cause they all kept coming around here, talkin' about how you were around there kicking it with yo' family and my dumb ass is sittin' on the porch like a deranged groupie or somethin'. Don't tell me you couldn't have at least called!" she ranted, eyes starting to well up with tears.

"You have no earthly idea what I had to go through to get that money to get you home, no idea!" she continued. "And then, when you said I couldn't come to the hearing, I was pissed at first cause she didn't even wanna come and get you out. But then, I had to understand that she rightfully comes first in all you do and that's cool, but damn! All I'm saying is that you could've at least sent word to me or somethin'!"

Her tears started to flow. She had finally gotten it out. The ranting was her way of informing Spider that he'd hurt her, something he said he'd never do. He placed his finger to her lips to quiet her down. No, he never meant to hurt her but she had to understand, he had shit to take care of on the home front. That was his safety net.

"Listen, Mommy, you gotta understand somethin' for me. I never meant to hurt you and I never wanna see you cry. Not from somethin' I caused. But sometimes, when muthafucka's feel like they got shit hangin' over yo' head or they know too muthafuckin' much of yo' business, they tend to get cocky. She was on my head right and left, every fuckin' move I made because she know I'm out on bail and she know that, all it takes is fo' her to start actin' ignorant and next thing you know, I'm gon' doin' hard time. It's the game... you think you surrounded by muthafucka's that always got yo' back but it ain't like that, baby.

Er'body uses this game to get what they want. To look out fo' number one. But I see different in you. I see somebody who ain't impressed by all the glory and bullshit. You just wanna be loved and treated like you deserve to be treated. And I wanna be that fo' you but you gon' have to understand that days like the last three days, happen sometimes fo' the reasons I just explained to you. But them days in no, shape, form or fashion, stops me from missin' you," he said kissing her on her cheek.

"Thinkin' 'bout you," he said, kissing her on the other cheek.

"Wantin' you," he said, kissing her on the lips.

He ran his hands up her thighs. She was wearing a stomach length teddy and a pair of shorts. He massaged her inner thighs.

"I'm sorry, baby. You know you my heart. I would never stay away from you on purpose," he said, touching her clit with his finger. Mystic fell into his touch.

"Thank you... thank you so much fo' getting me home. It didn't matter to me, who was in that court room at that hearing. I knew in my heart, who was responsible fo' getting' me outta there. I love you fo' that, lil momma. Look in my eyes; can't you see that?"

Mystic looked at him; becoming more and more entranced by his touch. She threw her head back and exhaled. It felt so good to feel his touch again. It felt even better, feeling it inside of her. He entered her slowly and told her to lay back. He moved her shorts to side. No time to remove them, he wanted what he wanted.

"I been dying to taste this muthafucka. It's all I could think about while I was there. The way that clit sits out. These big ass lips, hanging like cow pussy. I jacked off er' night, thinkin' about this pussy."

She lay back and thought of how different his touch felt from Remo's. She was debating on whether she should tell him or not. His tongue was so hungry, licking her in ways she knew only he could do. Her legs began to relax and Mystic let him devour her. He spread her lips apart with one hand and pinned back the skin from her clit with the other, exposing its hardness.

He wrapped his lips around it, took his tongue, wet it and slowly kissed it, as if he were passionately kissing her mouth. Mystic felt her body about to burst and he showed no signs of backing off. He kept it slow, which drove her even crazier and as her legs locked around his neck, he knew her time was near, she was cumming.

He applied a little force to her clit. Her legs began to shake as her body exploded. She moaned out in ecstasy and gripped his head with a death grip. She breathing so hard, she thought she would pass out. She decided right then and there, she wouldn't say a word about Remo, not then; not ever. She had her man back and that was all that mattered.

Spider removed his pants and boxers, towered above her; her panties still to the side.

"Thank you, fo' getting me back to my family," he told her, as he slammed inside her.

Bam!

"Thank you, fo' getting me back to my grind."

Bam!

"Thank you, fo' getting me back to my nigga's."

Bam! Bam!

"Thank you, fo' getting' me back to you."

Bam! Bam! Bam!

"And most of all, thank you, fo' getting' me back to my pussy."

Bam! Bam! Bam! Bam!

He pushed her legs back.

Bam! Bam! Bam !Bam!

He laid them across his shoulders.

Bam! Bam! Bam !Bam!

He forced them towards her chest.

Bam! Bam! Bam !Bam!

He had access, unblocked and free.

Bam! Bam! Bam !Bam! BBOOOOOOOMMMMMM!!!!!

He filled her with his gratitude and love. He lay on top of her and kissed her. He wanted her to know that no matter what he had to go through, from time-to-time at home, he would never leave her. She'd be his woman on the side, forever, no matter what.

"You still my baby?"

Mystic laid her face against his.

"Yeah, it's just…"

"Shhh, I got somethin' fo' you," he said, reaching down into his pants pocket on the floor, beside the bed.

He pulled out the tiny white box and handed it to her. Mystic eyes bulged at the sight of the gift. She couldn't believe he'd gotten her something. Every man knows, diamonds make everything alright, no matter, how big or small. Mystic opened the box and gasped at the ¼ ct. diamond earrings.

"Oh my God, Spider! Their beautiful!"

"Beautiful things, fo' my beautiful girl. You like 'em?"

"Yes, yes I do. Nobody's ever got me anything this nice before," she said, taking them out the box.

She quickly pulled her old earrings out of her ear, tossed them on the dresser and put her new diamond ones in her ear. Spider chuckled at her animation. He was glad she was happy again. He could focus on other things now but not before he got one more thing.

"Kiss him."

Mystic wet her lips, swished her tongue around her jaws to produce more saliva, leaned down, opened her mouth and began showing him, her appreciation for his present. She engulfed him and he loved it.

Mystic removed him from her mouth and straddled him. She began riding him with all she could muster up to give him. He gripped her thighs and held her tightly as she closed her eyes, arched her back and pulverized his dick with the muscles inside her.

As he moaned harder and harder, Mystic smiled. This was what she'd gone through all trouble for; all the drama… her man and the feelings he made her feel. She'd go through it again, she reasoned, if she had too. But Mystic needed to learn, be careful what you wish for, it just might come true.

Chapter Thirty Five

Cocamo spent Tee-Tee around and shoved her again through the living room. When they reached the front door, he pushed the tip of his pistol in the lower part of her back and told her to open the door. Tee-Tee couldn't bring herself to turn the knob. She couldn't face what she knew was waiting for her on the other side.

She shook her head "no." Cocamo pressed the gun harder into her back and told her again to open the door. Tee-Tee could no longer hold her emotions inside. She broke down and cried uncontrollably.

"Coco, don't make me do this. I have a daughter. Don't make my baby grow up without her mother."

Cocamo tilted his head and smirked.

"What the fuck? I don't have kids? Was you and that fat ass nigga concerned who the fuck was gon' take care of mines when ya'll plotted to kill me? Come on with that shit man, it ain't happenin'."

Tee-Tee stood at the door. She had to make him understand that she was forced to do this to him at first but that over time, she had come to care about him like she had never cared about anyone, except her daughter.

He gon' kill me anyway so fuck it! I'ma make him listen to me.

Tee-Tee took a deep breath, wiped her face, put her hand on the knob. That made Cocamo relax the pressure of the gun from her back, enough so that she could turn quickly to face him. He now had the gun aimed at her lower abdomen.

For a split second their eyes met and Tee-Tee continued to plead with him not to send her out the door.

"If you wanna kill me, just kill me. But don't let that fat nigga kill me. This wasn't suppose to happen like this, you and me. I mean, I was 'pose to get next to you, yes. I was 'pose to kill you cause you was takin' money out our mouths. But that was before…"

Cocamo didn't want to hear it. He raised the gun and moved closer to her face.

"Shut up! I don't give a fuck about anything you gotta say right now. You were just that loyal to that nigga that you had balls enough to think you could pull this shit off. At one point in yo' mind, you intended to kill me. As many times as I told myself not to trust yo' conniving ass, I fucked around…"

He couldn't bring himself to say he had fallen for her, hard. It would only cause him to hesitate in pulling the trigger when the time came.

"Say it, say it! You were about to admit that you didn't plan for this to happen either. Why can't you just listen to me and let me finish explaining."

Cocamo grabbed Tee-Tee by the arm and flung her around to face the door again. He once again demanded for her to open the front door.

Tee-Tee began to sob again.

"I can't, I can't… Coco please…"

"You think them crocodile ass tears mean somethin' to me? They don't!"

He reached around her, unlatched the lock and snatched open the door. He looked off to the wall. He too, couldn't believe it was ending like this. He had made a mistake in judgment that could've cost him his life. He knew he had to correct it and correct it, he would. It was them or it was him… and as he grabbed the back of Tee-Tee's shirt with his left hand and held the gun at her side with his right hand, his choice was both made and simple… it wouldn't be him.

Chapter Thirty Six

After making love for several hours, Spider and Mystic emerged from the house, on their way to Rally's to grab a bite to eat. When they reached the porch, Man was standing at the bottom of the steps, talking to Breeze.

When he saw Spider and Mystic. He shook his head. He moved Breeze to the side and asked Spider if he could talk to him for a minute.

"I got some business to handle and I need you to ride with me. You know, have my back."

Mystic didn't know why but she didn't like the tone in Man's voice or the look in his eyes. When Spider agreed to go with him, Mystic and Man made eye contact. She knew something bad was about to happen, she could feel it.

Spider turned to Mystic, reached in his pocket and gave her a fifty dollar bill. He told her to get something to eat from Dynasty's Market or John's Chinamen on West Florissant and Goodfellow.

"Keep the change in case I'm not back and you've gotta catch a cab to work. I'll be there to pick you up, aight?"

Mystic looked down at Man before she took the money from Spider.

"Where ya'll goin'?" she asked, more so to Man than to Spider.

Man just looked off to the ground and then back up to her.

"He'll be back, I just gotta handle somethin', and it won't take long. I'll try to have him back before you gotta be at work."

Spider grabbed Mystic by the cheeks and kissed her, hard on the mouth. Then he placed a soft kiss on her forehead. He walked down the steps and climbed in the jeep with Man. As Breeze and Mystic watched the jeep go over the hill of Mimika, heading towards Lillian, Mystic looked to Breeze.

"What's up with Man? Where is he takin' him?"

"I dunno, he said he found out somethin' about who killed his lil' cousin and he needed somebody to ride with him that was down fo' poppin' that thang. Supposedly, Spider knows the nigga," Breeze told her.

Mystic's stomach began to turn into knots and she felt nauseous. She hadn't been feeling well off and on, over the last few days but she figured it was just a loss of appetite, stressing over waiting to see Spider. But this was something different.

She went into the house, ran in the bathroom and threw up. Punkin came to the door, followed by Breeze.

"Bitch, that's the third time you done threw up in two days. Is you pregnant?"

Mystic turned on the faucet and rinsed out her mouth. She splashed water on her face and Breeze handed her a towel to dry her face.

"Me? Pregnant?"

"Bitch you fuckin' ain't you? And I know you fuckin' with no rubbers, so why the fuck not you!" Punkin told her.

"I don't think so," Mystic replied.

"Shit, I can't tell," Breeze snickered. "It shol' look that way to me. Shit bitch, you work at Walgreens, you betta use that discount to get you a pregnancy test.

212

Mystic washed her face and went downstairs to get her things ready for work. She sat down on the bed and thought about the possibility of being pregnant by Spider.

Pregnant? Me? I wonder what he'd say. Would he be hard since he's married. He's not gon' do anything to jeopardize his family. I just seen that. Would he leave me? Wow...me, pregnant?

She shook off the thoughts and continued to get ready for work. She would get a test and find out later. Right now, she was more concerned about Spider being with Man and she should've been.

Man headed down Goodfellow and towards Natural Bridge. He pulled into the Mobil Gas Station on the corner, bought a couple of beers and continued down to St. Louis Avenue.

He bought the jeep to a halt at Bare Brother's Park. Man told Spider to get out and walk over to the bleachers with him. When they took a seat on the grey metal bleachers over looking the softball field, Man handed Spider a cold Bud Light.

"Check this out nigga," Man began. "I asked you to ride with me cause I need to holla at you about somethin'. It ain't no business either."

Spider looked at him confused.

"Well, what's good?"

"I'm hearin' things on the streets. Things that I ain't dealin' with to good. We go along way back. We've done a lot of business and a lot of dirt together. But, I'm hearin' some shit that I ain't likin' to much right now. Me and you, we cool. I ain't never had no beef with you, right? So, man-to-man, I need to know, do you know who popped my lil cousin?"

Spider looked off at the ball field. Yeah, he knew. It was him but at the time, it was unavoidable. He couldn't tell Man that he had no choice but to fire at him because he'd drawn on him first. So, instead he lied to buy him some time to figure the shit

213

out. The streets were talking and he had to figure out a way to silence them.

"Fuck naw... who told you some dumb shit like that?" he asked, fishing for a name.

"That don't matter man, you said no, let's leave it at that."

Spider stood to leave.

"The other thing concerns Mimi. You know I love that girl like my own flesh and blood. Won't stand fo' shit to happen to her."

Spider looked down to Man.

"Fuck you mean? Ain't shit gon' happen to her. I got that, that's mine."

"Like I said, I ain't never had no beef with you. Until you sent somebody that I care about, out into a situation you know damn well, she didn't have no business in. Mimi don't know shit 'bout no muthafuckin' streets and you know it. I had to..."

"Hold on, Man. What you..." Spider attempted to interrupt him.

"Naw nigga, you hol' up. I had literally go pick *yo'* girl up from the gas station by O'Fallon Park at twelve somethin' at night. You know why?" Man asked, pulling out his strap and laying it on the bench.

Spider felt un-nerved because he'd left his, in his truck, parked back on Harney. He didn't know where Man was going with all this but he was starting to get pissed and quick.

"I had to go get her cause that bitch nigga you run with, picked her up from work and instead of him just taking care of the business you sent her to handle, this nigga pushes her fo' some head. She got the money but she ended up walkin' from *in* the park down to the gas station to get away from him. What the fuck he take her in the park fo' anyway?"

"Perez?"

"That's the nigga you sent her too, ain't it?"

Spider, bit the inside of his jaw. He hung his head down. He couldn't believe Perez had crossed him like that. Yeah, they were use to sharing rats but Perez knew how Spider felt about Mystic. He'd crossed the line this time.

He stood up on bench and told Man to take him to his truck.

"I need to see him," He said, pounding his fist inside his hand.

"That ain't it. I ain't done," Man told him, standing as well.

"When I finally got to her, she was on the verge of being robbed. She had a fuckin' knife to her throat. I have no doubt that the lil' nigga's tryin' to rob her was sent her way by yo' boy. I got one, beat 'em down, the other one took off. But even though it was handled, she had no business out there. Then, she…" he paused.

He was about to tell Spider about her little business trip but he decided against it. That trip had outer relationship consequences. She could end up back in prison if that information fell into the wrong hands. Instead, he decided to stay with the current subject.

"She cried like a baby when I got to her and I got on her head fo' being out there. Look, I know you do yo' thang with these rats out here, on the sly. But not this one, not her. She ain't built like that and she ain't like these lil' clucka's. She love you and if you ain't lovin' her back, or plan on shakin' some shit up to be with her; you need to step off and leave her the fuck alone."

Spider took offense to the tone in his voice, as if he was threatening him in some way.

"Aey, Man…"

"Naw, let me finish cause I need you to hear me clearly when I say this," Man said, stepping only inches from his face.

"I came to you outta respect. Cause I started to just cancel his bitch ass when I saw her goin' through that shit. But because I consider *you* peeps, I'm givin' you a chance to handle it first. And as far as Mimi goes, I suggest you handle that too. You do it or I'll do it fo' you."

Spider swallowed the lump in his jaw. He respected Man both as a friend and business partner. He didn't want to go to war with him, plus, deep in his heart, he knew he owed him this one because of his little cousin.

"You let me worry 'bout my pat'na… and my gal. I got 'em both."

Man sucked his teeth and nodded his head.

"You ready to head back?"

"Naw, you go on. I got some shit to handle. I'll get a ride."

Man reached in his pocket, pulled out his blunt, lit it up, picked up his gun from off the bench, placed it in his waist and headed for his jeep. When he pulled off, Spider pulled out his cell phone and called Tank. He asked him to come pick him up and to bring his piece along.

He called Perez.

"What's good, nigga?"

"What it do nigga, I heard you was home. You comin' through?"

"Yeah, I'll be there in a minute."

Chapter Thirty Seven

Cocamo stepped onto the porch, Tee-Tee close in tow. He looked across the street to where he had spotted Big Slug earlier and found him still sitting on Harney in the same spot.

He released Tee-Tee's shirt, dug in his pocket to retrieve her phone, which had been vibrating non-stop since he'd first removed it from her purse. He flipped open the Nokia and now it was Slug who was silent on the other end of the line. He could see Cocamo standing on the porch, with the phone up to his ear. He didn't know that Cocamo could see him as well.

Cocamo chuckled at the silence.

"What the fuck is so fuckin' funny nigga?" Big Slug asked him.

"I'm about to buss a muthafuckin' hole in my gut laughin' at you fake ass Bonnie and Clyde wanna-be's. Tell me somethin', how the fuck you gon' send a bitch to do a man's job? Naw, naw, I take that back cause I know why. Cause you just as much a bitch as this trifflin' muthafucka you sent over here to do yo' dirty work.

But I got a better idea, why don't you bring you' big, country fried chicken eatin' ass over here and finish it yo'self!"

Big Slug was furious at Cocamo disrespect but he also wasn't built like Cocamo. Slug was not the type of gangster to go toe-toe with a real gangster. He might send somebody else your way but he himself was all talk and unlike Tee-Tee and the rest of his street hustlers, Cocamo knew it.

Big Slug, still not realizing that Cocamo had him in his sights, continued to go at him, verbally.

"Nigga, you ain't said nothin' but a word. I run this muthafuckin' city! This here's *my* territory, my shit! Includin' that bitch you got on that porch. Bring it on nigga!"

217

Big Slug started his Suburban but didn't cut on his lights. He slammed the suburban in gear and took off, thinking he would catch Cocamo off guard. He rounded the corner at such speed, you would have thought he'd trained with Speed Racer himself. Cocamo didn't hesitate to move either. He threw Tee-Tee's phone into the street, reached around his back and pulled her gun from inside his waist.

"Move," he demanded, aiming her pistol at her head. She began walking down the porch steps. Big Slug's tires came to a screeching halt across the street from Cocamo's house. He jumped out his truck, with his .45 drawn and aimed towards Cocamo and Tee-Tee.

On the other side of the street, Cocamo was ready. One gun aimed at Tee-Tee and the other aimed at Big Slug.

"I guess here we go, huh? Some real Menace II Society shit. Go head nigga, this yo' territory, make yo' muthafuckin' move. Cause I'm letting you know, I'ma lay yo' bitch ass down."

"Nigga you and what army?"

"Me, Smith and muthafuckin' Wesson!" Cocamo told him, cocking the gun he had pointed at Tee-Tee's head.

You could literally see the steam rising from the top of both of their heads. The tension was so thick you could cut it with a knife. Tee-Tee stood there, legs trembling as if it was forty below outside. She didn't know who she should fear more. Big slug would hesitate to fire she figured because it was the possibility with Cocamo out the way, they could still get money together. None of his other street soldier's brought him the dedication to making money that Tee-Tee did. She figured that had to count for something.

Cocamo on the other hand, had nothing to lose by killing either one of them. She knew that at that moment he despised her for everything she had done and made him feel. He wanted to punish her, make her pay for invading his space… his world. It was Cocamo she feared the worst and she should've.

They stood there, two men in the game. Two men who would protect what they felt was theirs at all cost. Both understood they way it had to play out. Cocamo felt he was at an advantage because he knew Big Slug would never have the heart to pull the trigger himself. He would, if anything, stall until some young gunners he'd probably called, showed up. One thing was fact… one of them was going to the morgue that night.

Cocamo wasn't a man of many words when it came to other nigga's. So he spoke not one. His eyes stayed focused on his enemy's hand. One move of his finger and Cocamo would lay him down sideways. He also listened to the pitch in his voice. As his nerves lessoned, his voice would get stronger and deeper. Cocamo would know at that point, he'd have to make a move.

Tee-Tee stood there crying. Her emotions fazed neither Big Slug nor Cocamo. She'd have to answer to one of them or both of them. If she ever wanted to see her little girl again, she had to come up with something and quick. Her life and daughter was flashing before her eyes and as the commotion brought some of the neighborhood out onto the scene, Tee-Tee silently asked for help and she would get it, from a very unlikely source.

Chapter Thirty Eight

When Tank pulled up to pick up Spider, Spider was livid. He couldn't understand Perez's blatant disrespect for the game, let alone their friendship. His blood boiled as he filled Tank in on the situation.

"The nigga told my gal to give him some head in return fo' givin' her my money. *My* muthafuckin' money!" he said, slamming his fist against his chest. "How the fuck that nigga gon' play me like that man? This here been my nigga since Huggies, you feel me? And you'll cross me? Tank, nigga, I ain't never tried to holla at his bitch, neva!"

Tank covered his mouth and coughed.

"Could it be because she's built like Steven Jackson," Tank joked, trying to lighten the mood.

He knew Spider was ready to do something stupid and no doubt, something he'd later regret. Tank always believed that bitches were expendable when it came to the game. Unless it was your wife or your baby momma, someone you shared that concrete bond with, you don't step outside the box and create a war over a bitch. To Tank, they were like buses, if you miss one, in fifteen minutes the next one's coming. Why start all this shit over somebody you have no ties too?

Spider and Perez had done a lot of dirt together; they knew too many things about each other. Knew too many of each others dirty secrets. Rule #2 in the game, right behind the law of keeping your enemies closer than your friends, was pure common sense: Never go to war with someone who knows enough dirt on you, to burry ten feet deep. If you ain't trying to have your business put out in the streets or you're not trying to get set up or crossed out, you either sweep the beef under the rug and charge it to the game or you close their mouth with something stronger than glue… dirt.

Tank didn't want to see his childhood friends go at it over nothing or no one. He knew nothing good could come of it. Both had homes to protect.

"It ain't got nothin' to do with the fact that the bitch is only pretty from the knees down! Pussy ain't got no face and lips can't speak no wrong when they got my dick 'tween them. So it ain't got nothin' to do with how she looks but er'thang to do with respectin' the game.

It's about the boundaries you set and you don't cross. Boundaries set by the laws of the street. You don't fuck yo' patna's peoples, you just don't, The wages of that sin nigga, is death."

Tank gestured to Spider that he was about to pull over at the PX liquor store on Natural Bridge and Euclid. He wanted to grab a bottle of MD 20/20 to calm Spider's nerve. He returned to the truck with a six pack of Bud Light and a pint of MD. He popped the cap on the MD and handed it to Spider. He opened his beer and pulled off the lot.

"Aey man, you know I don't usually get in ya'll shit but I gotta say somethin' this time. How you know he told her that, man? She could've just said that, you know how chicks is nigga, they always wanna test you, see if you really give a fuck about them or not. Maybe she just wanted to see if you'd go to war with yo' boy over her and shit."

"She ain't like that," Spider said, shaking his head. "She didn't even tell me, Man told me. Perez bitch ass put her out by the muthatfuckin' gas station lot near O'Fallon Park. Man had to go pick her up and when he got there, she was bein' jacked by some lil' nigga's. She ain't tell me shit, which is why, I know he did it. And you'll put her out there for a muthafucka to try her? Come on Tank, nigga you don't do shit like that."

Tank took a swallow of his beer and belched.

"Yeah, I feel you. That was kinda fucked up. *If* it happened that way. Don't get me wrong, I like Lil' Momma, I just don't wanna see ya'll go to blows over this. We been hangin' to long fo' this. Why don't you just holla at him? Let him know that what he did was some fucked up shit. Charge it to the game, nigga. I mean, now you just know yo' boundaries with the nigga. That's what you said it was about, right? Now, you know you can't bring yo' girl or any female you get attached to around the nigga. Keep him close, right?"

Spider sighed a deep sigh and looked at Tank.

"I don't know man; I'm feelin' real antsy right now. I'm ready to hurt him."

"Well, I ain't ready to bury neither one of ya'll, nigga."

Spider took another swallow or the MD and handed the bottle to Tank. He popped the top on his can of Bud Light and stared out the window. His heart was beating so fast. He couldn't wait to face Perez. He felt so violated, so disrespected. In more ways than one, Spider would have preferred Perez had tried to fuck his wife, rather than Mystic.

He was so crazy about her. He loved her even more now for having to go through all that for him and still making it possible for him to come home. Loved the fact that she risked her own freedom and future to show him love and loyalty. He would return that love and loyalty by dealing with the one who hurt her, friend or foe, it didn't matter to him. He had to show her that he loved her and he needed her, just as much as she loved and needed him.

The truck pulled onto Cook Avenue and they exited the truck. Perez was sitting on his front porch, dress in a navy blue dickey short set and navy blue chucks, laid back in his wicker lounge chair, turning up a cold one. When Spider exited the truck,

Perez stood up and went to the steps to greet him Spider was stand offish, he remained at the bottom step, rejecting Perez's hand, that was outstretched to him.

"Later fo' all that, nigga. I'm hearin' shit in the streets, thang's that's got me all fucked up in the head right now. I'm sayin'   nigga,   I   thought   we   were   boys."

Perez looked at him, tilted his head and sucked his teeth. He wasn't feeling Spider's attitude and that put him on guard, instantly. He walked down the steps, around Spider and dapped up Tank, who was standing off to the side. He turned from Tank and stood face to face with Spider.

"What you mean, you hearin' shit and I don't know, are we boys? Fucks wrong with you?"

Spider looked Perez in the eyes and from the vibe Perez got from Spider, he knew that Mystic had told him what happened. Perez exhaled and looked off at the ground. He was outside naked. His gun was in the house. And even though Tank had dapped him up, he knew that what ever way it went down, Spider and Tank was the closest, Tank would ride fo' him. He was out gunned and out matched, so he backed down but not for long.

"I been hearin' some snake shit on the streets. Shit that I know ain't fo' me and you. Or least I thought it wasn't." Spider said, taking a swallow of MD. "I'm tryin' to figure out what the fuck was you trippin' off of, when my gal asked you fo' *my* muthafuckin' money, that you asked her fo' some head, nigga?"

Perez jerked his head back and threw his hand up at Spider, playing it off, as if he knew nothing about what Spider was talking about.

"Man, what the hell? I thought you had heard some shit about me settin' you up or somethin'. I know muthafuckin' well,

223

you ain't come over here to question me about some shit a bitch told you!"

"First off, she ain't a bitch; watch yo' mouth. Second of all, she ain't tell me. A lil' bird told me muthafucka. So what the fuck is that about? That's how we do it now? We cross each other's boundaries? Ain't no limits on what the fuck we can do now? Let me know, cause I'm sayin' yo' peoples been tryin' to gimme that ass fo' the longest."

Perez walked up to Spider and stood toe-to-toe with him.

"My man, you drunk, so I'm a let that slide but nigga, don't you ever let that shit come out yo' mouth again about my peoples."

Spider thought about all the years they'd been friends but then he also thought about Mystic and how eyes bucked when she'd seen his gun for the first time. How it had scared the shit out of her. How scared she must've been when the lil' nigga's were trying to rob her. It infuriated him even further.

"How 'bout this," Spider said, moving only inches away from Perez's face. "Don't you fuckin' go near her again, fo' any reason or it's whatever, nigga. And me and you, we gon' continue to make this money together cause we do it well, but homie, don't test me. You know me, I know you…it's both of us or neither one of us."

Tank stepped in between them. The conversation was going somewhere he didn't want it to go. Perez put his hands up in the air as Tank pushed them apart from each other. Perez chuckled at the thought of going to war with Spider. He had saved his ass too many times in the past to fear him. Oh sure, he knew Spider would get down but not to the point where Perez, would ever have to worry about him in that way.

Perez walked back up the steps and sat back down in his wicker lounge chair, picked up his beer and put it up to his lips.

"Oh yeah, speaking of money and business, I'll have that fo' you later on today. Wouldn't wanna ruffle yo' feather's any mo' than they already are. But as far as taking that trip back to Indy, you might wanna think that through befo' you go." Perez said, taking a swallow of his beer.

"Really? And why is that?" Spider asked.

"Cause, while you over here, questioning me about that lil bitch...oh, my bad.... that chick of your's, you might wanna address ya boy in Indy. From what I hear, he actually did fuck her."

Spider walked up the steps and stood over Perez.

"Nigga, get the fuck outta here with that shit! She ain't took her ass to no muthafuckin' Indy. She can't even go outta town, nigga. She on probation. So, I know that's a muthafuckin' lie. She ain't finna drive up to Indy and ride back with no dope. So what, you ain't get none and now you tryin' to set her out there like a hoe?"

Perez was getting real tired of Spider stepping up in his face, trying to defend a woman. He rose up out the chair and sat his beer down on the wicker table beside him. He looked down at the ground and then, he placed his hand on Spider's chest and pushed him backwards against the porch rail.

"Nigga, you got one mo' muthafuckin' time to get up in my fuckin' face and fuck it, we can do this shit real gangsta like. You on some bullshit over a bitch! Yeah, I called her a bitch!"

Tank was holding Spider with one hand to his chest and Perez with his other.

"Chill nigga's!"

225

"Naw, fuck that, Tank! He wanna be all whipped and shit, then let him hear what the fuck kinda bitch got him whipped! She didn't drive no where, she took the greyhound up there, fuck that nigga for that dope *and* paid him *yo'* muthafuckin' money, nigga! Now how she moved that shit and got yo' ass out, I don't know but I can call that nigga Remo right muthafuckin' now and let you hear it fo' yo' self."

Spider snatched away from Tank and turned away to face the front yard.

No way. She wouldn't have?

Then he thought back to the day he kept calling the house for her and Breeze kept telling him she was out with a friend and didn't know when Mystic would be home.

"Call him."

Perez took out his cell phone, put it on *speaker* phone and dialed Remo's number.

"Yo' don't say shit," Perez told Spider and Tank. "He'll spit freely if he thinks it's just me."

When Remo answered the other end of the phone, Spider's attention fell solely on the voice coming through the speaker.

"Yo', yo', whad dup son?" Remo greeted Perez.

"Shit nigga, chillin' on my front porch, with a brew in my hand. I'm thinkin' bout makin' that trip this weekend."

"You already know, its good son."

"Yeah. I'll be makin' it by myself. My nigga still inside," Perez baited him.

226

"Aw yeah, I guess that bitch took that Cush and did her own thang, huh?"

Spider stepped closer to the phone and Perez put his hand up to him.

"Yo', I still can't believe she rode to Indy on the bus fo' that nigga. *And* gave up the pussy? Man, that's some deep shit."

"Shit, you know I don't like da nigga anyway fo' real. So yeah, it was taxes on that shit. Although, she tried to act like she wasn't wit' it but she gave it up freely and loved every stroke of it." Remo said, snickering through the phone. "She might be waitin' on that nigga to come home but I know fo' a fact, she thinking 'bout this good, you heard me?"

Spider's blood had reached its boiling point. His anger turned to Mystic.

How the fuck she gon' do me like that? Actin' like she so in love with a nigga and she fuckin' my connect?

He looked to Perez and wondered if he too, had scored that night before he put her out of the car. Remo's voice had totally faded to him and all Spider could see was Remo, entering Mystic and Mystic made the whole robbery thing up just to cover shit up.

He could see his face, pits and crates, brushing up against her skin. Did she dig her nails, deep into Remo's back as she did his? Did she lock her legs around him the same way she did when Spider plowed deep inside her? Did she talk to him and whisper the same sweet shit in his ear? He needed to know.

He hit Tank on the chest and motioned for him to leave. He shot Perez a look that told him, this situation wasn't over. Perez knew Spider expected his money from him, now more than ever. Perez gave him a quick nod of the head and continued his conversation to Remo.

As Spider and Tank drove away, they could hear Perez cracking up in the background.

"That's one bitch-ass-nigga!" Spider spat out.

Tank decided to keep his comments and thoughts to himself this time. There was nothing he could say to his long time friend to make this one better.

Spider finished off the MD and stared off into space. Everything he'd felt for her had gone out the window with the empty MD bottle he threw. He wanted to hurt her and hurt her, he would.

Chapter Thirty Nine

A small crowd began to gather on the scene. Punkin, Mystic, Get Down, DC, Breeze and Unc. The rest was Tee-Tee's hustling peers, Toi, Hank, Lil' Curtis and Harvey. Although they were all down for making money together, Tee-Tee didn't expect help from any of them. None of them were going to stand up to neither Big Slug nor Cocamo; this she knew and they certainly wasn't going to take a bullet for her.

Lil' Curtis looked at Tee-Tee and saw the tears coming down her face. He knew then, that what Tee-Tee had told him was true about what Big Slug had wanted her to do. From the looks of it, Lil' Curtis assumed, the plan had gone all wrong.

Big Slug saw the crowd gathering and thought to himself.

I gotta make an example out of these muthafucka's. If I let them slide, everybody will attempt to try me. Especially Tee-Tee, she got workers under her and if get a pass, the rest of them nigga's will think they can fuck up too and not have to pay the price for disobeying my orders.

Cocamo focused on Big Slug. He watched his body movements and noticed he was looking around at all the people gathering around them.

This nigga might try to get some balls about his ass since muthafucka's is lookin'. He might be tryin' to stunt cause he don't want er'body to know what I know… that he's a pussy fo' real.

Cocamo was ready. He moved closer to Tee-Tee and stood sort of behind her. Big Slug stepped back on his right leg and placed his left hand underneath his right hand, which was gripping his .45.

Lil' Curtis stepped to the side of Cocamo.

"Man, this shit here ain't even necessary. Coco man, Why is you out here trippin' with this fat ass nigga?"

Cocamo didn't respond but Tee-Tee did.

"Lil' Curtis man, gone on back on the side walk. This shit ain't got nothin' to do with you. I don't need you tryin' to clean up my mess."

"We fam, Tee. And you know I know what the fuck is goin' on. All this shit goin' down cause that fat, punk ass nigga, didn't have enough heart to bring the noise to Coco himself."

Cocamo tilted his head towards Lil' Curtis' voice.

So this nigga knew she was planning this shit, too?

He couldn't turn towards Lil' Curtis because he had his guns positioned on the two they needed to be on. But he did take the time to address him.

"Nigga, you knew what the fuck these muthafucka's was up to? You knew this shit the night you came to my crib to bring this bitch's purse and you ain't put me up on game? After all the shit I done gave yo' monkey ass over the years? You'll play me, too?"

"Naw, Coco man, it wasn't even like that," Lil' Curtis said, taking a step away from Cocamo.

Big Slug chuckled.

"Nigga, I'm gon' say it again. These here ain't yo' streets, they mine's! These simp ass muthafucka's round here know not to bite the muthafuckin' hand that feed them. This ain't no game we playin' here. We in this bitch to win this bitch.

Nigga from day one, that bitch had yo' number. She was down to take you off the map for me. Loyalty nigga; that's what you gotta have in this game. Muthafucka's that are so scared to disappoint you and depend on you to the point where they'll rob, steal and even kill fo' you. Ain't that right Tee-baby?"

Tee-Tee looked down at the ground.

"So, this was what all the questions was about the day RJ knocked on my door? You was trying to find out shit to report back to this fat greasy muthafucka? I should splatter yo' muthafuckin' weave all over this muthafuckin' concrete right now!"

  Tee-Tee looked to Big Slug and bit down on the inside of her lip. She knew at that moment that Slug had no intentions of trying to save her. He had just handed her over to Cocamo's anger on a plate. He had plans to get rid of both her and Cocamo. So since she figured she was gonna die anyway, she might as well take Slug with her.

Fuck it, let him kill us both.

"Yeah, that's what it was all about. I was recruited at first to take you out 'cause this nigga said, you was stealin' our customers; takin' bread out my pockets and food out my mouth. He told me you was runnin' around the 'hood talkin' shit that you couldn't back up and he wanted yo' mouth shut, permanently. At the time that was all I could see, surviving out here in these streets and taking care of my daughter. But once we started hang…"

"Ain't no need to go off all into that," Cocamo interrupted. "From day muthafuckin' one, you stepped in my house on a mission to do this shit fo' this nigga. You was adamant about doin' this nigga's dirty work. Now that yo' shit got twisted, you want me to hear you out and go down memory lane with you. Fuck that! Yeah, I tripped… you caught me slippin' but now, it's whatever."

He looked to Big Slug.

"And I mean, whatever!"

"Naw man, Coco man, listen to me. Nigga I walk around here bullshitin' everyday, all day. But right now man, I'm so serious. Yeah, Tee-Tee told me what the nigga was up to the night she got locked up. She showed up, face swollen cause the fat muthafucka slapped her for not movin' fast enough in handlin' this shit. That's gotta say somethin' right there. She cut fo' you, she told me that night, that's why I brought her purse to you. She told me she had feelings fo' you."

Cocamo was unmoved.

"Then," Lil' Curtis continued. "The big pork smellin' ass nigga pulled a gun on her in front of my crib earlier cause she still hadn't took care of you when you got her out the Justice Center. So, think about it, if she really wanted to go through with this shit, don't you think she would've done it by now? Or at least tried it by now? Do you think she would've kept takin' all that bullshit from that shit from that nigga or just handled her business and snuffed yo' ass out?"

Unc walked over and leaned in his nephew's ear. He knew Cocamo. He knew that blood shed was inevitable and he wouldn't go down without a fight. He didn't want to see his nephew in trouble but he also understood, it had to go down, one way or another.

"Think this shit through, Neph. Don't lay yo' life down over somethin' you can live to battle against another day. This that same girl you was just on the couch, wondering if you wanted to kick it with fo' life. Now, I ain't sayin' you shouldn't handle yo' business here. I ain't sayin' you shouldn't put no muthafucka six feet deep. I'm sayin' make sure it's the right muthafucka and fo' the right muthafuckin' reasons," Unc told him.

Tee-Tee felt the ending about to climax. She could hear it in everybody's voice and she could definitely feel it in the air. Someone was about to die and it was probably her.

"Nigga, didn't I tell yo' bitch ass to stay out my muthafuckin' business?" Big Slug asked Lil' Curtis.

Lil' Curtis put his hands up in the air and took a step to the side.

"Aey man, you ain't gotta holla! I smell that muthafuckin' fat back comin' up from yo' stomach. Nigga so fat that when you spit, you spit out Canola Oil. When he sweat, you can wipe that nigga with a rag and then polish yo' furniture with all that muthafuckin' Lard comin' out his pores."

The crowd laughed and Big Slug was both embarrassed and pissed off. While Lil' Curtis thought he could take some of the tension out the air with a little humor, he actually just made it worse. Big Slug got in his emotions quick and before anybody knew it, he swung his .45 over towards Lil' Curtis and fired.

Cocamo didn't wait to see who or what was hit. He fired... it didn't matter which pistol in his hand went off...he just started squeezing the trigger. The sounds in the air, were like World War II. Everybody started running, screaming and hiding. Ducking behind anything that could shield them from all the bullets flying from one side of the street to the next.

When it was over, two bodies lay on the ground. Both gasping for air, both unsuccessful. Blood was flowing through the streets, tears were falling from familiar faces and two of the 'hoods most unforgettable people....were dead.

Chapter Forty

Mystic stared down at the stick she'd just urinated on. She focused on the *plus* sign that digitally appeared in the capsule. She was pregnant.

How would he react, she wondered. What would he say? Would he ask her to get rid of it because of his situation at home? While she was afraid of his reaction, slowly, she was becoming excited within herself. The thought of another life growing inside of her was making her ecstatic. Especially since she'd lost her little girl. She rubbed her stomach and smiled to herself.

Wow, a little Spider!

She had to find the perfect time to tell him. She wanted it to be special. Maybe have him take her back down to Union Station by the water, where they went on their first outing together. He would be shocked, she expected that but she also knew that ultimately the loyalty she'd shown him while he was locked down, would play in her favor. Eventually, the thought of them being bonded together by blood, would make him happy.

Mystic understood that he already had a family and she would never try to jeopardize that, nor would she allow her too. She was satisfied just having her very own piece of the man she had come to love.

She picked up the phone and dialed his number. When he didn't answer, she hung up the phone. She never left messages on his machine because from what he told her, his wife was the kind of woman that would just sit and play with the numbers until she finally figured out the code to his answering machine.

Mystic called six more times over the next couple of hours and all six times, he didn't answer nor return her call. She was getting worried until his knock came at her side window around eight o'clock that evening.

When she went upstairs and opened the door to let him in, she instantly knew that something was wrong. He had a look on his face that startled her and when she leaned in to kiss him and he turned away, Mystic knew that the nauseous feelings in her stomach were right.

"Hey daddy," she said, smiling as he entered the door.

"We gotta talk," he responded, walking past her.

"What's wrong?" she asked him, following him in the basement to her room.

Once inside, he closed the door behind her and locked it. Mystic sat down on the bed and looked up at him. Her heart was racing a mile a minute with thoughts of anticipation. Her gut told her it was something to do with his wife. Maybe she had found out about them, she didn't know.

Spider was pacing back and forth in front of her and she was getting more nervous by the minute.

"Bae please, tell me what bothering you?"

She stood up and step in his path, bringing them only inches from each others face. He looked at her and realized at that moment, he hated her. Hated her for making him care for her. Hated her for making him feel like he was her everything. Hated her for making him need her... for making him love her.

It didn't matter to him that he was married. That to Spider, was a whole separate part of his life. Common sense would have told him that he had no right to be upset with her for whomever she chose to sleep with, but the game just didn't go like that. Mystic was his and his alone, regardless of the fact that he had a wife. The worst thing she could have done, in his mind, was make him look like a fool in the streets.

"The day I couldn't find you when I was locked down and I kept calling and yo' sister kept tellin' me you were out with a friend... where were you?"

Mystic looked off to the wall and sighed. Remo had spilled his guts and now she had to figure out how to defend herself in a way spider would understand.

"I don't know what you mean... I was... uhh.. out tryin' to get together yo' bond money."

"And just how did you do it? I never asked cause it was obvious to me that you just did what I'd asked you to do. But apparently you had other plans. I took you outta town with me cause I wanted you to know that part of my life and to show you that I trusted you."

He chuckled.

"*Trusted* you."

Mystic reached for his arm.

"You can trust me baby. What are you talking about?"

"Seems to me like you liked more in Indy than just the food. You saw a reason to go back without me. You fucked that nasty dick nigga! That lame, broke ass nigga! You fucked a nigga that I deal with in my business? That deals with me?"

"All of this shit is a lie and the way you actin' ain't fair."

"Fair?" he repeated, towering above her. "Fuck fair!"

Mystic grabbed at his arms as he snatched them away.

"It wasn't like that, Spider he's lyin'."

"Ah, so you *were* there?"

Spider shoved her out the way and headed for the door. Mystic jumped in between him and the exit.

"Yeah, yeah I was there but I had no choice. I went to Perez like you said and he," she began to cry.

236

"He wouldn't gimme all yo' money! Then he said he would if I gave him oral sex. When I wouldn't, he put me out the car and I had to ask Man to come and get me. When he got there, some boys were tryin' to rob me. I didn't have enough money to get you out, so I figured I would go to Indy, get some weed from Remo, bring it back and then have Man get rid of it, quickly. That was the only way."

"Get out my way!"

Mystic shook her head.

"No, no I won't let you go! You gotta believe me! I rode the greyhound up there. Remo was supposed to meet me at the station. But when he got there, he said the police was riding tough so he'd left it at his room. We went to the room and..."

Spider was biting the inside of his jaws and ready to strike her at any moment.

"When we got to his room, he showed me the stuff, I gave him the money but then he wouldn't bag it up. When I told him I had to go, he told me that if I wanted to leave with what I came fo', I needed to give him what he wanted."

"Move the fuck out my way, Mystic!" he snapped at her, pushing her to the side.

She held her ground and continued trying to explain.

"Don't you see, I couldn't leave there without it! I was already there illegally. If I got caught outta town, I'da been in jail. But I needed to get you home. I needed that weed to make it happen."

For the first time since he'd been downstairs, he looked at her. Stared into her eyes and Mystic thought finally, she was getting through to him. She placed his hand on her face. Spider tried his best to feel what she was trying to tell him. But all he could see was Remo touching her, Mystic's facial expressions, her voice and it was all too much for him.

He needed to get away from her. He was ready to put his hands on her for making him look like he didn't have any control over what was his, to Remo. She made him look soft and weak. He couldn't handle that.

"How you think I'm supposed to go back there and do business with them? I look like a damn fool! Where am I supposed to find a new connect, huh? You disrespected me... you disrespected yo'self! Did you think about how that shit was gon' look and affect me when I got back home? You fucked that nigga! Did you fuck Perez too?"

Mystic's eyes widened and she shook her head vigorously, no.

"Yeah, I know 'bout that, too. Now get the fuck out the way, I'm not gon' ask you again."

Mystic held the knob with both hands behind her back. Spider grabbed her by the shoulders and this time, he used his force to literally throw her out of his way. He walked out the door and Mystic grabbed him around the waist. She tried to hang on for dear life, crying and screaming for him to believe her. He slung her to the right and she hit the wall, hard.

"Leave me the fuck alone! Don't call me, don't text me, nothin'! We done! You feel me, done!"

Mystic grabbed her side and bowed over onto the floor, crying uncontrollably. The pain in her back was excruciating. She never got the chance to tell him her news. And now, it seemed as if she never would.

"He hates me!" she cried. She couldn't understand why it was her, he was upset with. His boys had crossed him, not her. In her mind, she was doing whatever she had to do to get him home, to be with him. She thought he'd love her more for that... she was wrong. She remained balled up in the fetal position for hours. She couldn't stop her heart from hurting. She didn't know what to do next.

What am I gon' do? He won't talk to me, he won't listen to me. He don't wanna hear nothin' I gotta say.

She clutched her stomach with one hand, placed her head against the other and cried.

Other Novels by Allysha Hamber

Unlovable Bitch, A Hoe is born

Keep It On The Down Low, Nobody Has To Know

What Done in the Dark, Will eventually Come To Light

The NorthSide Clit

Available at: www.Amazon.com
Contact the Author at:
Lele4you@Hotmail.com
www.facebook.com/allyshahamber
www.myspace.com/diamondclit
allysha4you@yahoo.com

Coming Soon:

The NorthSide Clit II

Unlovable Bitch II, A Whore's Revenge

The Clean Up Man

LaVergne, TN USA
19 November 2010
205624LV00007B/59/P